THE MIND MASTERS

THE JON KIRK OF ARES CHRONICLES

THE MIND MASTERS

THE JON KIRK OF ARES CHRONICLES, BOOK FOUR

GARY LOVISI

A Scientific Romance inspired by Edgar Rice Burroughs'
John Carter Series and set upon the faraway planet Ares

WILDSIDE PRESS

Published by Wildside Press LLC.
www.wildsidebooks.com

CONTENTS

THE PEOPLE & PLACES IN THE JON KIRK OF ARES CHRONICLES

ALUN KIRK: the son of Emperor Jon Kirk and Lady Sirah of the Green Empire of Ares. At this time he is still a baby boy but he will become as great a warrior as his father.

AKAR GORM: Captain of the Enemy Empire warship *The Attara*, aka *The Destructor*, who defeated, joins forces with Jon Kirk.

ANCIENT BOOK OF KOR: a mythical lost tome said to possess the super-science of the ancient people of Ares.

ARON THE ELDEST: elder and mind-power master of the Old Ones of Keva. The leader of the Mind Masters.

AR-DEN: ancient wise man and one of Jon Kirk's most important counselors.

ATTARA, THE: warship in Lord Doom's space fleet commanded by Captain Akar Gorm. The name of the ship translates to *The Destructor*.

BLACK DRAGONS, THE: mounted riders and warriors who are the body guard of Emperor Jon Kirk.

BLUE KORTAS: alien blue-skinned horned mercenaries, large mutant well armed killers not native to Ares and brought in to fight for the Secret Empire. Now allied with Jon Kirk under their leader General Zod.

BRAN: one of the Secret Empire prisoners and a pirate from the planet of Ko-Ah-Leh who befriends Jon Kirk.

CALIAT: one of the six green cities on the continent of Cos on the planet Ares occupied by the Zaran Winged-men and then set free by Jon Kirk and Tar-gool, renamed Tarcos in honor of Tar-gool.

CALI-NOR: a mystical realm or city that to the Greens of Ares most closely approximates their version of our Heaven.

CAVES OF CONSCIENCE: a huge network of caves north of Tarcos in the Coastal Mountains that Jon Kirk used as his headquarters during the invasion of Ares.

CAXIL: Gorm word for a dirty rat-like creature that lives upon his planet, an insult.

CONSIGNATS: impressed fighters, or slaves, forced to fight for the Secret Empire of the Hundred Worlds.

DARK NIGHT: Flagship of Lord Protector Doom leader of the Secret Empire fleet in orbit around Ares.

DARK SPHERE, THE: the mind land or soul of all the people of Ares who had ever lived—a kind of universal mind in the Ares concept of Heaven, the Cali-Nor. It is dangerous to contact and difficult to control.

DAUNTLESS, THE: Jon Kirk's flagship, captained by Kevnar, a female felina.

DEATHRAY, THE: Ares space warship commanded by Gorm of the Gorms.

FIGHTER, THE: Ares space warship commanded by Tor-nul.

GENERAL ZOD: military leader of all Blue Korta empire shock troops.

GORM: of the Gorms, a large Viking-sized alien who befriends Jon Kirk.

HE WHO IS NOT TO BE NAMED: also known by the words Kin-Ty-Roo, said to be Emperor of the Known Universe and master of what is called the Enemy Empire, which is locked in a vicious war with the Secret Empire of the Hundred Worlds ruled by the Sindaki Lords.

HUNDRED WORLDERS: short name for minions of the Secret Empire of the Hundred Worlds, also known as the Secret Empire, ruled by the Sindaki Lords.

JON KIRK: Emperor of the Green Empire of the Six Cities of Ares and Earthman hero, husband to Empress Sirah, father of Alun Kirk.

KAL-SAR: Imperial governor of one of the Six Cities who defied Jon Kirk's order to evacuate his city and fought the Blue Kortas. His entire army and civilian population was massacred by the enemy.

KEV: hidden city on the western continent of Ares. See Keva.

KEVNAR: Captain of *The Dauntless*, a female felina. Jon Kirk's flagship.

KEVA: ancient hidden city of the Greens whose people have great mind powers, destroyed by a ship of Lord Mentep's fleet and later rebuilt and renamed Kev in a secret location on the western continent of Ares.

KIN-TY-ROO: words to indicate the being called Emperor of the Known Universe, the words roughly translate into the phrase "He Who Is Not To be Named", but this being is a complete mystery but is master of what is called the Enemy Empire.

LARL: Mythical ancient Ares youth, son to hero Ry-Nar who entered the body of the dread Zarbane monster to retrieve his body.

LORD PROTECTOR KARLATH DOOM: Lord Protector and leader of the Secret Empire of the Hundred Worlds fleet in orbit around Ares. His flagship was *Dark Night*. Doom is a Sindaki, a race who is said to have unnatural mystical powers.

MANALIA: wife to Zaor, Jon Kirk's most trusted friend and general of the Green Empire army of Ares.

NEWCOMERS: general name of the minions of the Enemy Empire troops under the Kin-Ty-Roo or Emperor of the Known Universe.

POLN: female *felina* tiger creature who befriends Jon Kirk.

QUARTO: Winged-man from Zar who is the captain of *Dark Night*, the flagship of Lord Protector Doom of the Secret Empire of the Hundred Worlds, later becomes Admiral Quarto-Zar of the fleet.

RAS-NOOR: Ares scientist, associate of the great Tar-gool, master scientist of Ares and the man whose machine brought Jon Kirk from Earth to Ares.

RY-NAR: Ancient Ares warrior hero who entered the dread monster Zarbane to retrieve the body of his son Larl, much in the manner of Jonah and the whale on Earth.

SAHN-JOR: friend of Jon Kirk and the First Minister and administrator of the Green Empire of Ares.

SECRET EMPIRE, THE: known as the Secret Empire of the Hundred Worlds, interplanetary empire of which the Winged-men from Zar are a part, a very small part, and which is seeking to reestablish Zaran rule on Ares and enslave the greens-skinned humans and destroy Jon Kirk and his Green Empire.

SHAMAR: young king of the mind-powerful people of Keva, later he is king of Kev, and a friend to Jon Kirk.

SHARN: Leader of the alien Tergats and sub-commander who runs the control room of the prison ship *Solar Happiness*, and who joined with Jon Kirk.

SASHEEN: merman from the sea world of Talu who befriended Jon Kirk.

SHORNS: a religious sect on Zar whose Winged-men adherents believe in peace and non-violence. They do not eat meat or people. Captain Quarto is a Shorns.

SIRAH: Empress of the Green Empire of Ares and wife to Earthman and Emperor Jon Kirk. Mother of Alun Kirk.

SLOSS: Ares word for garbage, or lies.

SOLAR HAPPINESS: prison ship of the Secret Empire captured by Jon Kirk and his companions.

TAMBU: a Gorm from the planet Gorm who is a blood brother and companion to the huge Viking-like alien creature called Gorm.

TAR-GOOL: an old man, master scientist and patriot of the green-skinned humans of Ares, friend of Jon Kirk. He was killed in the battle to free the city of Caliat from the Zaran Winged-men, the city of Caliat was renamed Tarcos in his honor.

TERGATS: race of tall, gangly yellow-skin humanoids with fins under control of the Secret Empire. Sharn is a leader of the Tergats.

THREE FORMS OF POWER, THE: The Ancient Ares philosophy of the three actions of warfare, encompassing the Physical, Super-science, and the power of the Mind Masters to defeat an enemy. Used by the Sindalki to take down the Ancients of Ares and to found the Secret Empire of the Hundred Worlds.

TOR-NUL: Captain of Emperor Jon Kirk's imperial bodyguard, the Black Dragons.

TRONTA: young Keven stationed as a mind master on *The Dauntless*.

VALLADONT: Admiral Quarto-Zar's flagship, which in the Zaran language means 'battle ready'.

VUL-CAN: Ancient Ares colony world located between Mars and Jupiter, long ago destroyed by the Sindalki and now forming the Asteroid Belt.

WINGED-MEN: the brutal flying creatures from the planet Zar who have terrorized, murdered and eaten the green-skinned humans of Ares for millennia, also called Zarans.

ZAOR: Jon Kirk's most trusted captain and best friend on the planet Ares, brother of his wife, Sirah. General of the Green Empire army.

ZAR: home world of the Winged-men, one of the planets in the Orion star system.

ZARBANE: a mythical massive vicious monster of ancient Ares texts. Heroic Ry-Nar entered such a beast to retrieve his son Larl's body.

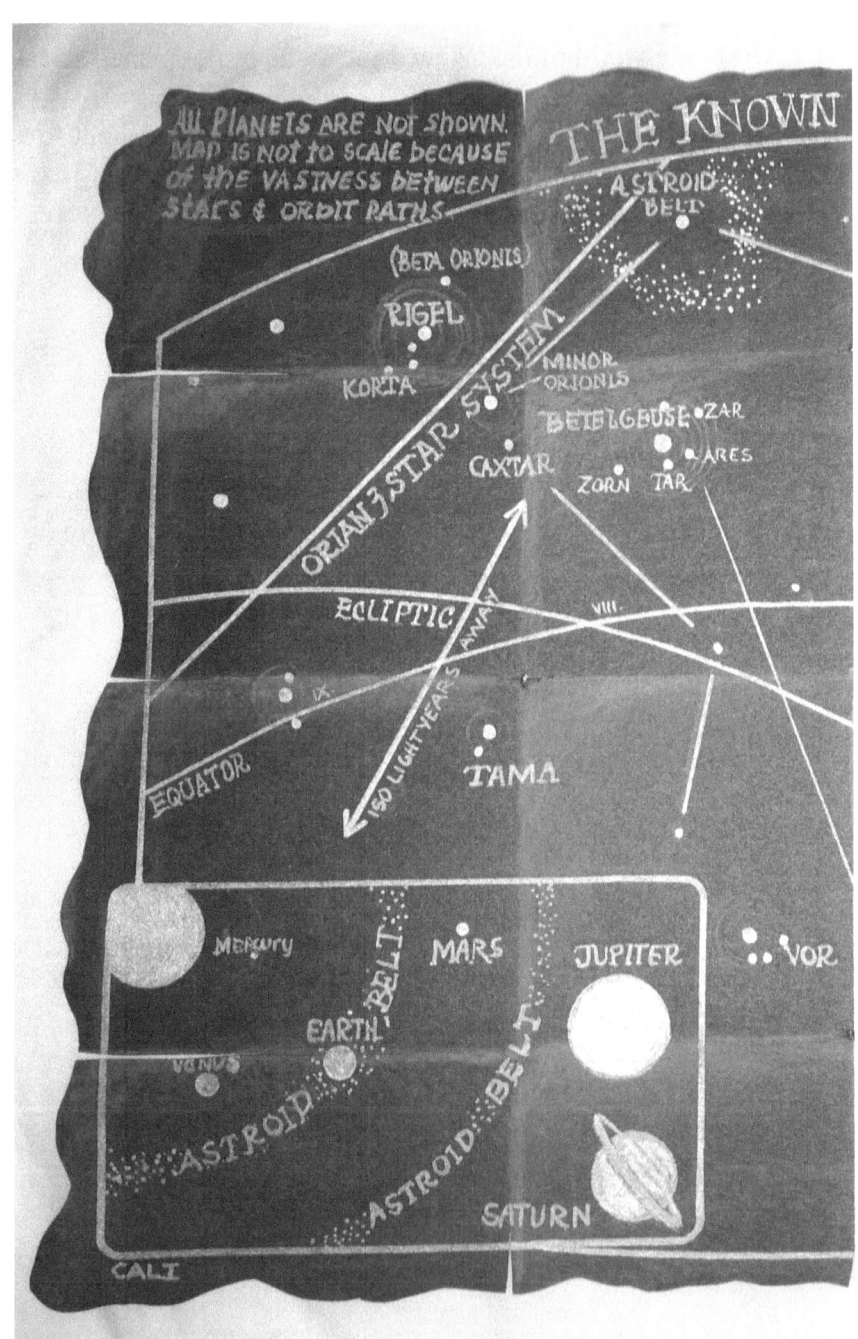

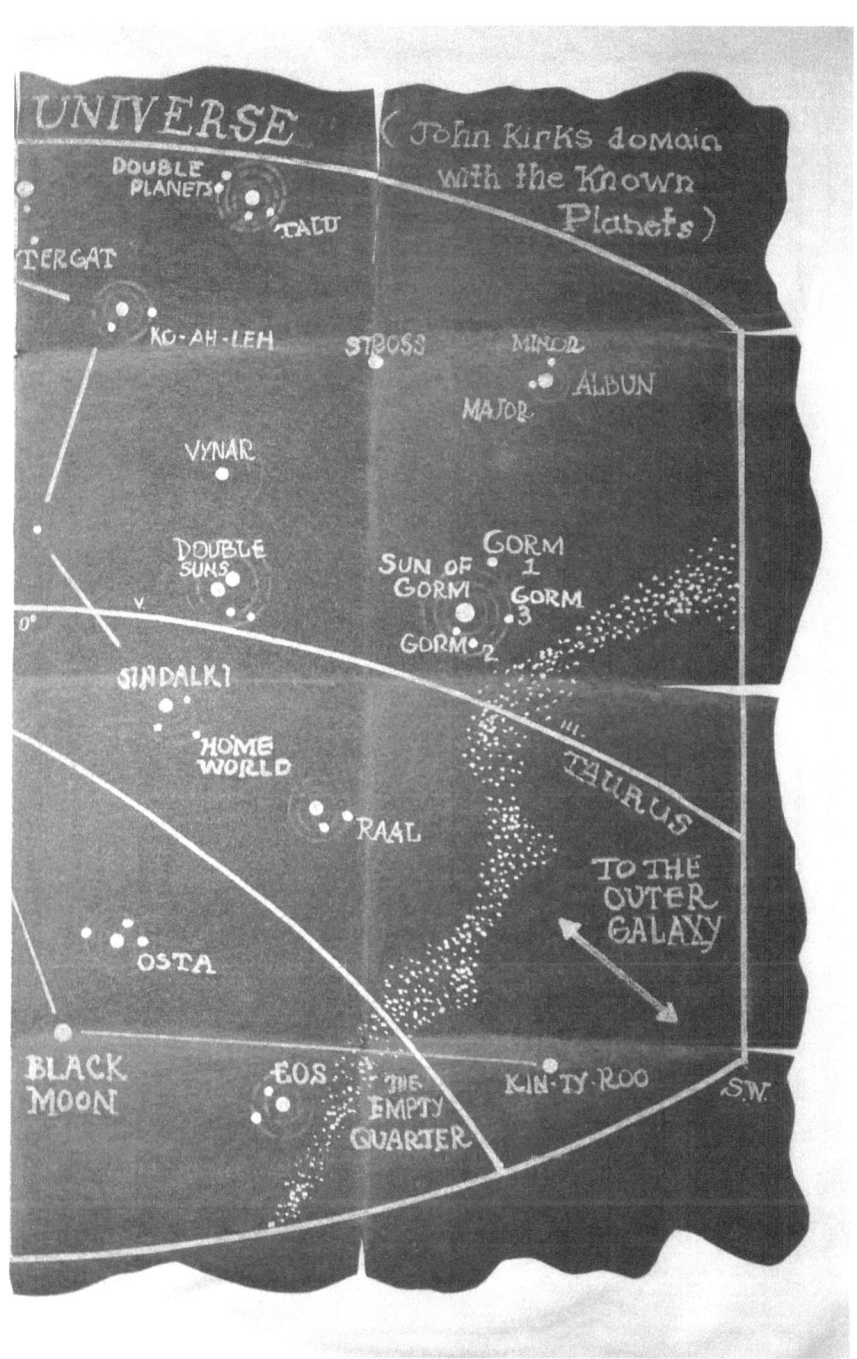

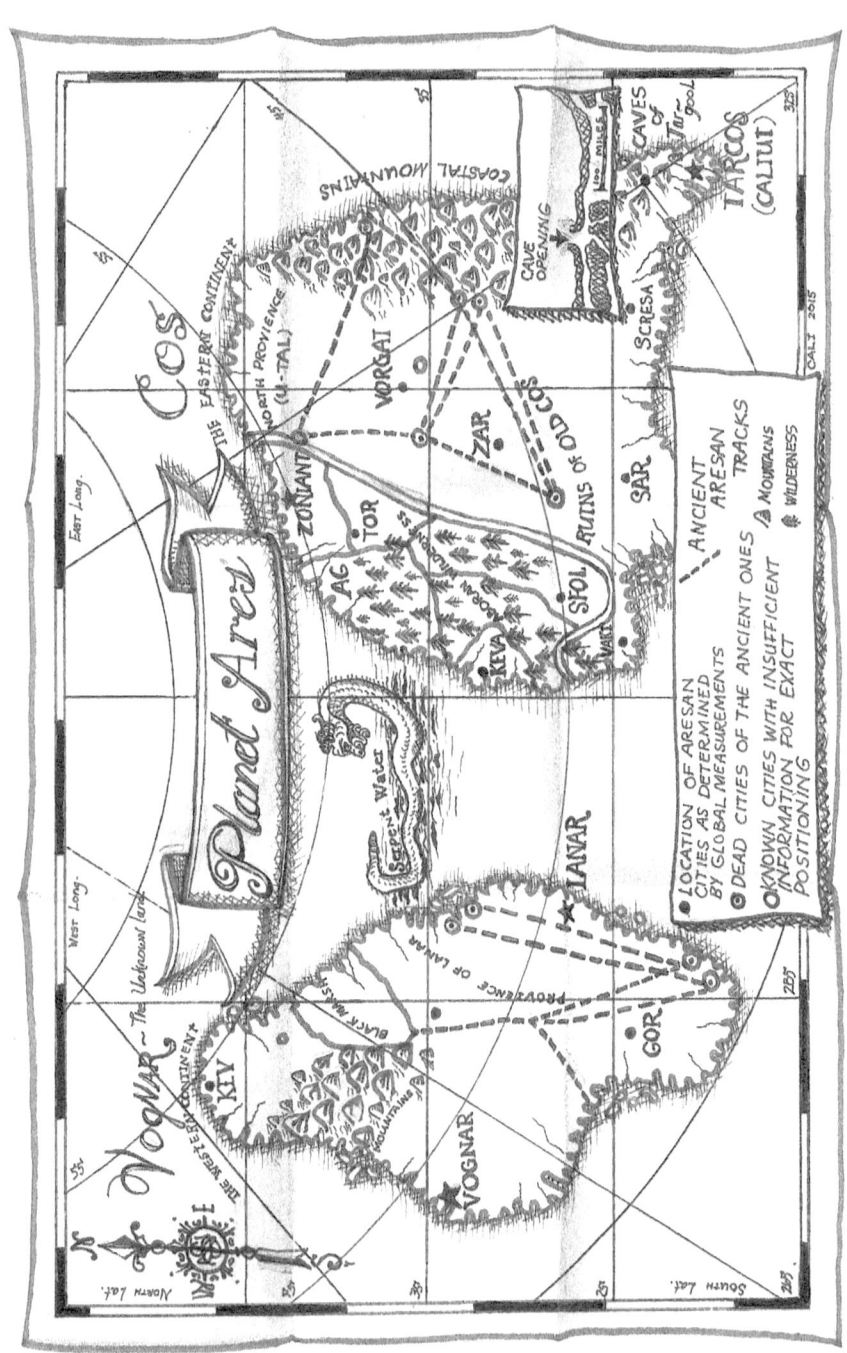

CHAPTER 1

Space Battle

Three enemy warships were quickly hurtling towards Ares. They were not trying to disguise or hide their attack. They were opening coming on—hard and fast!

Great danger was on the way and our defenses were now in an uproar. The alarm was immediately sounded throughout the palace and the fortress in Tarcos where I ruled our fledgling empire. All pretense of my much-vaulted emperorship was gone from me now as I ran furiously towards a speedy flier that was parked on the palace roof waiting for me. It would blast me and my companions into the upper atmosphere to escape the gravity of Ares and get us to my warships that were stationed in low space orbit protecting our world. Along with me were two of my most trusted comrades in battle; the commander of my Black Dragons bodyguard, Tor-nul; and Gorm, the huge Viking-like warrior from the world of Gorm.

"Only three enemy ships?" Tor-nul asked me in evident surprise, as we entered the small planetary flier. We got in quickly and belted ourselves into our seats. Then I immediately hit the starter and piloted the small craft in a fast upwards arc towards the fleet of dozens of our mighty warships stationed in protective orbit around Ares.

Tor-nul continued with his questions. "Why would the enemy attack Ares with only three warships, Jon Kirk? What is their game?"

"I do not know," I answered grimly as I operated the controls.

"Hah, well it is obvious, they must be spies. Or perhaps advanced scouts to probe for weakness?" Gorm stated his question with his usual gruff grumble. He did not think too much of these enemy ships, nor of the enemy. I knew better.

"Or they could be the vanguard of a vast fleet coming to crush Ares. The enemy has the ships, thousands of them, I have heard," Tor-nul added grimly.

"Or it may be some kind of suicide attack?" Gorm spoke up more sternly.

I nodded, I had thought of all these possibilities of course, but I had no idea yet what this was all about. Not yet, but I was sure we would all find out soon enough.

I accelerated the tiny flier to full speed throwing all caution to the winds. We would be at our orbiting warships soon, the crews of which having already been alerted by Admiral Quarto-Zar, so I knew they were standing ready and impatient to take off to meet the oncoming enemy in battle. Then whatever was to happen, would happen.

"We will crush them all!" Gorm, of the mighty Gorms told me in a halting grunt with his usual defiant confidence. He was angry. He did not like this situation at all. He seemed to take it as some kind of a personal insult—to himself—or to me. I could never decide which, with Gorm. He was a unique kind of fellow.

The three incoming ships were the mystery now. They might be some kind of secret spy run, or even a suicide attack. Maybe the enemy thought they could sneak in three ships under our defenses to do us damage? Maybe they had been found out via Ras-noor's excellent sensor devices? Perhaps it really was some kind of suicide attack? I could not say for certain yet, but we would go out to meet these enemy ships and either capture or destroy them. We had no choice. We must protect Ares.

My friend Gorm, the huge Viking-size warrior just shook his head in anger, "Lord Doom is behind this, the dirty *caxil* is playing with us. He is playing with you, Jon Kirk, testing our defenses. He sends in three ships to see what we will do. Suicide ships to take our measure. Whatever you do, Jon Kirk, do not send our full fleet after these ships if they run from us. They may very well be sent here to lure the fleet away from Ares. That would leave the planet defenseless."

"Ares is not defenseless," I stated, thinking of the many large and powerful platform ray projectors ringing the mountain tops of both continents of my adopted world. I looked at Gorm and smiled, he had called Doom a *caxil*, which in his language was a dirty rat-like creature. It was a great insult for a Gorm to call anyone such a name.

I nodded to Gorm, acknowledging his insult to Doom and the fact that I would never leave Ares defenseless.

Gorm just grunted, he did not like this bold incursion into our area of space by three enemy warships, and he did not place much trust in ground-based planetary defenses.

I nodded at him, "Gorm, I understand, but we have to meet this threat, and we shall. Zaor, Sahn-jor and the others will remain upon Ares. Quarto will remain in command of our war fleet and keep it in protective orbit around Ares. You and I, and Tor-nul here, will each take command of a warship and take it out to meet these three invaders in a one-on-one space battle. Then we shall see what they are up to."

"That is good, Jon Kirk. Too bad Zaor is not here to join in on the fun." Gorm offered me a wry grin, and then with a loud laugh he added, "And I shall tell him all about what he missed afterwards."

"Yes, I had the devil of a time convincing him to stay behind—for if I am wrong and we do not return—he will be needed to lead the empire—and to protect Sirah and Alun."

Gorm grunted, but gave me a knowing confident smile.

Tor-nul nodded gravely, he was not always so confident, he knew defeat was always a possibility. He also did not like any type of flying, especially here out in space. He was the commander of my elite Black Dragons bodyguard, the bravest of the brave but they were a planetary military force, not a space-going force. They were not yet, at any rate, but I had plans to change their mission in the future—that I had not told Tor-nul about yet. They would become a version of our new Space Marines. For now, however, I could see my young friend was quite nervous about flying through the atmosphere of Ares, and now, ever upward into the darkness of outer space in a high orbit around Ares where the massive warships of our fleet were on station. We could see them now. They were enormous, bristling with weaponry. We moved in closer. Slowly. Careful.

Admiral Quarto-Zar's voice came over the comm. "My Emperor, this is a dangerous mission you are to embark upon, I do not agree to it, you are placing yourself in severe danger. Allow me to send someone else."

"No one need risk their life," I told him firmly. "I will go and do what I must do."

"I still do not agree with this, Jon Kirk," my admiral replied, then insisted, as if his instance would change my mind on the matter. It could not. I would never send out anyone on a mission and into danger that I would not face myself.

"You do not have to agree with me, Quarto, I understand your feelings on the matter, but I will not risk any more than three of our ships to go up against three of these enemy ships. And I will not risk my people, other than these volunteers. I will also not risk having our fleet lured away from Ares, so hold fast, while we advance upon this threat and determine just what it means."

"Yes, My Emperor." Quarto's voice came over the comm, and if a monstrous Winged-man could show the emotion of sadness or regret, I could feel it then in his voice. It was a touching moment, coming as it was from one of his kind.

Until a year before I had hated the Winged-men of Zar, who had invaded and controlled Ares for so many centuries—hated them all with a burning passion and rage. I had killed many of them, including two of their major leaders. Since then things had changed drastically. Now I knew one of them whose honor and respect I held in great measure and trust. Ares was a most alien world and always full of surprises for me.

I brought our tiny flier close in towards the airlocks of the three warships we were to take to meet the invaders. Our ships were ready, the crews armed and waiting. I dropped Gorm off at one of the ships, *The Death Ray*, and Tor-nul off at *The Fighter*, and then I took the flier over to my flagship of the small fleet, *The Dauntless* and then entered the huge vessel.

Captain Kevnar, a female felina was in command and greeted me warmly, "Jon Kirk, My Emperor, we are ready. My ship is your ship."

"Your ship is your own, Captain, but I am thankful and happy to hear all is in readiness. Please see to it that all three ships leave Ares and our small fleet immediately advances to face the enemy at full speed. We have no time to waste."

Kevnar smiled, showed her sharp and pointed feline teeth in anticipatory glee at the oncoming battle. She had been a *consignat*, an indentured warrior, sold as a fighter, like so many others who crewed the old Secret Empire warships recently controlled by the now dead

Sindalki masters. All but one of them being dead now—and that last remaining Sindalki was Lord Karlath Doom, a monster and my deadly nemesis! He was not only a danger to us all, he was a great traitor to his own people! I was sure these three enemy warships approaching Ares were from his own large battle fleet. What was their mission? Our three ships sped out to intercept them in the emptiness of space before they came too close to Ares.

"Tor-nul, Gorm?" I spoke into the comm, from my position near the captain, in the control room of my vessel, *The Dauntless*, my voice coming to them on their own ships.

"We are here, My Emperor, our ships are ready and our weapons loaded. We are positioned right behind you," Gorm grumbled, he too was anticipating a grand space flight with a glorious battle at the end of it. The Gorms were a most war-like space-faring race, once conquered by the Secret Empire and held under the control of the hated Sindalki for many centuries, now their leader and their people were part of my new empire and they had proved to be most valued warriors. Gorm of the Gorms, their leader, had also grown to be a good friend to me. He was a bit rough around the edges, as were all his kind, but he was an able warrior and a man I trusted and greatly respected. You could not ask for a better friend, other than my best friend since I had come to Ares, my wife's brother, Zaor.

"Good, then full speed ahead!" I replied, my mind full of grim thoughts, running all kinds of scenarios over in my mind, wondering what we were to find when we met these three enemy warships. I knew we would find out soon enough. "Move out until we make contact. No further communication between us. As soon as we get within range we go to invisibility and then use all our weapons to destroy the enemy ships if they do not surrender immediately."

I looked around the bridge and saw one of Lord Aron's mind masters, a thin youth named Tronta, who even for his young age was said to have great mental powers. He was stationed upon this ship, while two of his fellow mind masters were on the other two ships of my companions as well. So we were well covered from mind attack. The mind masters were essential, for we were going up against Lord Doom, or his minions, which meant deadly Sindalki mind powers would be in play and they could be vast and devastating. We needed our own mind masters to repel whatever lethal forces they might throw against us. And while I was sure Lord Doom was not himself on any of these three oncoming enemy warships, he certainly had agents with mind powers on them to do battle with us upon that plane of mental power and thought energy. I knew what we were dealing with and I hoped we were prepared.

"Enemy sighted!" Captain Kevnar told me in a sharp voice, and the alarm came out to us from our other two ships now too. "They are nearby and moving in to close with us!"

"Acknowledged. Go to invisibility," I ordered quickly to all three of our ships.

"Yes, it is done," Captain Kevnar replied.

I nodded, then shook my head in evident distress. I noticed that the three enemy warships had gone to invisibility as well. Now our invisibility did not matter, for our sensors could see their ships just as well as if they had not become invisible—and they could see us just as clearly as well.

"Well, our invisibility is useless to us," I stated grimly. It had once been our secret weapon courtesy of the Blue Vognars, but now it had come into such common use in war that it had become useless. Military secrets are the most fleeting of all. We had to find another way to defeat this enemy without the aid of invisibility.

"Move in closer, ready the death ray beams and our projectile cannons," I spoke to the commanders of all three ships.

"Ready! We await your orders to fire, Jon Kirk," the captain of *The Dauntless* told me. Tor-nul and Gorm on their ships also told me their vessels were ready and in a position on my flanks and set to fire. Waiting for the word and the first target.

I wanted to hold off until the enemy came in closer before we opened up on them and then we would hit them hard. The enemy was less patient. Less accurate as well.

The three enemy warships were quick and fired first, impatient, thinking to get in the first licks. Devastating rays of intense heat and fire, flame and death, inconceivable forces of gravity and extreme mass, forces that until I had come to Ares I had never thought possible hit us very hard—but our shields were strong and held firm. We immediately returned fire upon the enemy warships and hit them back just as hard. The harder. Devastating powers slammed into their three vessels from our most powerful weapons. Terrible weapons of great power. The forces in play were incredible. But our shields held and our other protections, compliments of our three mind masters, stymied their attack on the mind control plane against our officers and crew. Their mind masters could not effect our people. Our powerful defense was weakening their attack. Our shields held their physical weapons in check so that for now, their death rays, projectiles and other weapons were ineffective against us.

Once our ships were closer and in position I ordered a complete counterattack with every weapon we had. It was devastating. We hit them with everything that we could use against them. Death rays, projectiles and beams of all types smothered the three enemy vessels, completely enclosing them in a whirling vortex of fiery energy and bright white light. It was terrible and amazing to see, it seemed that no ship—no living creature—could ever survive such an overwhelming onslaught. But when I ordered the attack to cease, we saw that our weapons seemingly had no effect upon the enemy ships. It was uncanny, amazing, terrible, but the enemy ships looked as if they had not been damaged by our fire at all. Their shields had held and they appeared undamaged.

The battle, for all its use of incredible deadly energy and immense power had done little damage to either side and become a stalemate.

I knew a full mental onslaught by the enemy mind masters upon us was next. The enemy had mind masters of their own onboard their warships—as did we. They were not of the caliber of Aron of Kev, nor of Lord Doom, thankfully, but they were powerful and they would seek to use their mental powers to infect the minds of my crew, and even enter the computer system that helped to control our three vessels. Then they activated their power to the full against us.

Captain Kevnar could see the signs and spoke up in alarm, "Here it comes!"

The onslaught of powerful psychic energy hit us all like a hard slap in the face, and it would have effected us a lot worse if not for our own mind masters onboard each of our three ships, who fought back every attack with one of their own. Now Tronta, and his companions on our other two ships resolutely gave as good as we got from the enemy. Their powers checked the enemy force. Then they gave back more force, even harder. The mind master attack by our enemy seemed to resolve into another stalemate.

"They are stymied, Jon Kirk," Tronta of Kev told me and Captain Kevnar with obvious pride, "their powers are checked. The enemy has substantial mind powers, but ours are more than equal to their own, and they are unable to penetrate our defenses."

"That is good," I looked at Kevnar and Tronta with relief as I thought fast about what my next move would be. What to do? I knew I had to act fast.

"We are closing on the lead enemy warship, Jon Kirk," Captain Kevnar reminded me. "That should be their command ship, or flagship."

I nodded, I knew what we had to do now. It was a big gamble, but I was all about taking big chances when necessary.

"See to it all our crew is ready, and inform *The Death Ray* and *The Fighter*, that they be ready to take immediate action. We are going to board the enemy and take their ships!"

"Yes, Jon Kirk!" and the captain quickly gave the commands. In moments all seemed ready from our end. My three ships moved in close to each of the three enemy ships. It was do or die now. Time to give the order that would lead to victory or death.

I knew it was a dangerous call, a big risk. I knew it was a reckless chance I was taking but I could see no other path to victory now. Warfare, in seemingly all aspects, upon all three planes of power, had become a stalemate at this point. Both sides had the power of invisibility—and had counter measures to render it ineffective. Both sides had the same particle beam and death ray weapons, projectors, all that could be rendered ineffective with powerful shielding. Even nukes could be rendered ineffective by the powerful shielding. Both sides also had their own mind masters who controlled devastating mental powers—but each could stop the other in battle and render these powers also useless. Ineffective. Impotent. There seemed to be no way to beat the enemy warships out here in the lonely darkness of space—except the old-fashioned way. Hard fought physical force and that had to be done hand-to-hand. We would use that now!

"Captain, let us get ourselves down to the dock immediately and join the rest of your waiting crew. I know they are armed and ready to board the enemy vessel. Alert *The Death Ray* and *The Fighter* to be ready to send their boarders away as soon as they make contact with their target ship!"

"Yes, Jon Kirk," Captain Kevnar replied as she put her ship controls on automatic. Then armed and with her crew behind us, we were ready to take our positions to board the enemy ship. The bridge was on auto, for every hand was needed now in the hard fought action to come.

"Contact made!" the captain shouted in a fury of wild anticipation, "the docking mechanism is in place and connecting our ship to the enemy ship preparatory to boarding!"

"Good!" I shouted, waiting, anticipating. The airlock now automatically cut open an entrance through the enemy shielding and then, the though the hull of the enemy ship.

"Connection made, shielding down, the hull is breached, Jon Kirk!" Kevnar stated triumphantly.

"Now open the portal and follow me!" I shouted as I ran into the body of the enemy warship, being the first one on our side through the airlock portal into the enemy vessel. I charged ahead with my short sword pointed outward in one hand, and my trusty Colt .45 Auto in the other. I got off five fast shots, bringing down five enemy soldiers as I advanced, and my crew advanced right with me. I rushed into a corridor of the enemy ship, met another full dozen enemy warriors, swords and ray guns out and firing, as I and my crew fired back at them. Many fighters on both sides wore small personal shields that blocked death ray beams, but they could not block the sharp blades of thrust and slashing swords. So the battle was fully joined now and blood was being spilled.

It soon became a loud, terrible, bloody spectacle of severed limbs, flashing swords, searing death rays, and the acrid odor of hot burning flesh. The sound, light, and smell was terrible. We fought on, pushing the enemy back, taking a terrible toll on their numbers. It was obvious they had never expected such an attack and were not trained to repel boarders in hard hand-to-hand fighting. Most members of both crews wore small portable shields, that protected them from death rays and from some projectile weapons—so it was now down to swords, daggers and axes on both sides—weapons that shielding could not protect against.

I saw Captain Kevnar cut down two of the enemy quickly. She was a positive battling dynamo in a fight. Even mind master Tronta, who I kept by my side to look out for his safety, fought well and he took down a charging enemy warrior with his sword—though I am sure he used some of his mind powers to dull the wits of his attacker to make his fight a bit more even. Whatever his reason, he won his fight and I was thankful. I took down the next enemy who was coming at him from the side, then another enemy tasted my blade as he tried to sneak around my guard to outflank us. I blocked him and took him down quickly. The battle was pressing us for all we were worth.

I was pressed for time also, but I quickly wondered how Gorm and Tor-nul were doing in their battles with the two other enemy warships as they boarded them from their own vessels, *The Death Ray* and *The Fighter*. I wondered what was happening on my two other ships as I and my crew fought for our lives here to capture the enemy flagship.

This is what happened on the other two ships, as it was told to me afterwards.

* * * *

Gorm of the Gorms commanding *The Death Ray*, under Ship Captain Ular, growled in red rage as he hefted his huge battle ax and with a wild shout led his boarding party onto the enemy warship through a breach in the metal hull.

"Follow me, lads! We're taking this ship!" Gorm barked and the officers and crew of *The Death Ray*, armed to the teeth like Earth pirates of old, surged onto the deck of the enemy warship. A breach had been made through the enemy shields and then through the hull of the enemy ship to allow entrance. The airlock held the atmosphere secure.

Gorm's boarding party surged into the enemy vessel. The two armed forces met in a wild melee and battle raged with all manner of deadly weapons. The two forces clashed at the opening where the airlock allowed access by Gorm's warriors into the enemy ship. The defenders tried to stop them from coming aboard. Resistance here proved heavy at first, but soon enough became lighter as things were quickly sorted out in the heat of bloody battle—the defenders were outclassed and many were soon killed. The enemy moved back, fearing the raging attackers. This seemed to be a good result and Gorm pressed his apparent advantage. It seemed to presage his victory until the real reason showed itself to Gorm. He noticed one of the enemy officers running forward with what looked to be some type of grenade—something that could destroy the airlock connecting the two ships—and probably both ships as well. Gorm knew it had to be an explosive device of some type—or perhaps the gods forbid—some type of hand-held nuke? If that was true, they were all doomed. Was it some kind of suicide attack?

"Stop that man! Bring him down now!" Gorm shouted, pointing out the enemy officer as the man tried to get away to set off his device, but one of Gorm's boarding party quickly took the enemy officer down. Gorm's man was able to get the device out of the enemy officer's hands before he was able to complete implementing the code that would set off the grenade. The bomber was brought down and held down so that he could not move.

Gorm was there in a heartbeat moment and quickly took the grenade from his men, looked it over carefully, growled in relief that it apparently had not been activated, and then deftly dropped it into a nearby disposal chute in the corridor of the enemy vessel. Let them worry about it, he thought. The grenade was apparently not armed and thankfully it did not go off. It was instantly disposed of out in space. For that Gorm was most grateful, but soon his attention was needed elsewhere because his crew needed help to clean a swath through another corridor of enemy defenders. Gorm whirled his massive war ax over his head in a fearful spectacle of bloody rage, as he led his boarding party deeper into the enemy ship.

The enemy defenders were now giving ground, and their captain, a seemingly wily fellow, had retreated with all the remaining members of his crew into the security of an engineering control room. Gorm's men quickly took out the security door and surged into the room with a relentless and resounding fury. They were eager for victory now. They could taste it in the air, along with the odor of the blood that had been spilled. Here a larger pitched battle was fought as the two sides charged into the huge area and went at each other with swords, death ray blasters, and projectile weapons. Bodies were cut and torn by sword thrusts and rending slashes; flesh was roasted or melted by death ray beams where the victim did not have a proper shield, or a personal shield was not in working order; while the hull of the ship was wracked with dozens of small holes from the many projectile weapons fired by both sides.

Luckily, the ship's shields held, and the repair mechanisms of the ship's hull controlled by the onboard computer were able to maintain the air loss and pressure changes created from damage by the weapons discharged in the battle. Smaller projectiles could not do the ship serious damage even if they went through the hull—but Gorm knew that if an enemy had another grenade, then they were in trouble. So he urged his attackers quickly onto victory before that might happen. Time was of the essence.

"Cut them down! Do it quickly! Take no prisoners other than unconditional surrender!" Gorm shouted as he struck down one of the most valiant defenders with his ax blade. The man was cleaved from breast to thigh and fell down in a mass of horrible red flesh. It was terrible. Gorm shook his head sadly at the waste of brave life brought about by this battle, which made him only fight on all the harder and vigorously to achieve victory, in an effort to end the carnage as soon as possible.

Gorm led his boarding party forward against the last dozen enemy defenders who seemed to want to go down with their ship in some kind of suicidal frenzy. While this was not desired by the mighty warrior, if left with no choice, Gorm would surely accommodate them. He urged his men forward, and led by his mighty war ax, the attackers made great headway into the flagging enemy. Suddenly the enemy captain threw down his blaster and sword, bowed his head and submitted.

"We surrender!" the enemy captain shouted, quickly ordering his remaining crew to throw down their weapons with his own. They obeyed him immediately. "It is over!"

"Yes it is!" Gorm shouted in obvious relief. The carnage was ended.

Gorm lowered his bloody battle ax, ordered his men to take the enemy crew into captivity, and after sending a small party of warriors to capture the bridge—where they only found two defenders who gave up immediately—he was soon told that the entire enemy ship was under his control and that all fighting had now stopped.

It was good news. Winning this battle left a good taste in Gorm's mouth, and even though it had been hard fought and bloody, victory was always preferable than the alternative. Gorm suddenly growled a loud victory cry that was taken up by the rest of his crew and boarding party that rang out resoundingly throughout both ships.

* * * *

Meanwhile, Tor-nul, commanding *The Fighter*, had come upon the enemy vessel that was his target in a sudden and surprising hard and fast broadside. The two warships clashed, hulls smacking upon each other, their straining shields rubbing up against each other in a loud ominous groaning of metal and other even more bizarre sounds.

"Get those shields down! Bring down their shields!" Tor-nul ordered sharply, and the captain of *The Fighter* nodded and immediately gave the order. He was a wily Tergat, who had already given the commands so that his crew was ready for what was to come.

"Enemy shields down, My Lord!" the Tergat captain shouted to his commander.

Tor-nul nodded, he was a fighter, but he was one not accustomed to fighting out here in the vastness of outer space, and he was not comfortable being addressed as 'My Lord', so for a heartbeat, he did not reply to the captain of *The Fighter* who was talking to him so forcefully.

Tor-nul allowed a grim smile, he was a 'Lord' on this vessel as far as the captain and crew were concerned, he could scarce believe it. He nodded and just hefted his death ray rifle, set his personal shield to 'On', then gave the order, "Lower our shields and connect these two ships. I want every member of this crew armed and ready. Set your personal shields, and take your place at the center airlock, then prepare to follow me into the enemy vessel, upon my command."

"I have already given the order, My Lord," the Tergat captain replied smartly, as he and his bridge crew set their automatic controls, then they picked up swords and death ray pistols and followed Tor-nul down to the center of their ship and into the airlock that was now being set to connect the two vessels.

An engineer near the airlock saluted Tor-nul, spoke up briskly, "Sir, we have just breached the hull of the enemy warship. It is open now and ready to be boarded."

Tor-nul allowed a grim smile, looking forward to action. He hefted his death ray rifle, and then shouted to the crew, "Follow me! We are taking this ship now! Boarders away!"

Tor-nul led a surge of all the warrior crew of *The Fighter* into the enemy warship. There were met by an initial wall of resistance by a dozen hearty defenders led by the enemy captain, but these were quickly shot down, or cut down, by the relentless fury of the attack of the boarding party. Under Tor-nul's leadership the boarders fought like fiends, for they liked and respected this young officer who was the commander of Emperor Jon Kirk's famed Black Dragons bodyguard. None would disappoint him in battle this day.

"They are falling back! Now we press the attack! Follow me, men!" Tor-nul shouted as he led his boarding party to push their attack harder and ever forward. They were relentless. They tried to give the defenders quarter, but the enemy would not yield or surrender. Brave fighters, but foolish, so Tor-nul gave the order to push the attack to the ultimate end and take down the last of the ship's defenders if they would not surrender immediately. It did not take long.

Once that battle was over and won the ship was now defenseless. The few remaining enemy crew hiding throughout the ship surrendered to Tor-nul's men immediately and without a fight. The bridge was found to be deserted, the controls left on automatic, so a member of Tor-nul's crew was tasked with regaining control of the ship and setting the new course. It was not long before the enemy warship was completely under the control of Tor-nul and the crew of *The Fighter*. He quickly notified Jon Kirk, who was still fighting his own battle from *The Dauntless*.

* * * *

Suddenly incoming calls came over on my comm, "Jon Kirk, this is Gorm, *The Death Rays* have taken the enemy ship—it is now ours!"

I heard a wild cheer come over the comm from background voices behind Gorm. Then another voice I recognized spoke in a loud excited tone.

"Jon Kirk, this is Tor-nul, the crew of *The Fighter* have taken the enemy ship we were tasked with, the defenders have surrendered. The ship is now ours!"

More cheers rang out.

"You have both done well!" I told them, for this was very good news. Now it was time for us to make the big push here. "Captain, you and your *Dauntless* warriors, let us take this ship! We will take our victory now!"

A cheer went up from the crew as they followed me forward to clash with the enemy. This Enemy Empire ship was far larger than the other two and held more defenders, so we were more closely matched here. It was taking us longer to win through, but I knew we would do so. We fought hard to push the enemy defenders into a narrow corridor where they were soon trapped, and then we came at them with a fury they could no longer resist.

The captain of the enemy warship now having found out the news of his other two ships having been taken and surrendered accepted the new reality and suddenly dropped his weapons. His sword and ray pistol fell to the metal floor of his ship with a loud clang.

He looked over at me sharply, "Jon Kirk, I surrender to you. My crew and my three ships have done all that was required by us, and for our honor, to fight against you. Now we surrender, and await your punishment."

I looked carefully at the enemy captain. I noted that he was another Gorm, a huge hulking Viking-like warrior, grim and bold. I knew that he did not like surrendering. He reminded me very much of my own friend, Gorm. Why was a Gorm fighting with Lord Doom? Then it came to me.

"You are a *consignat*?" I asked him carefully.

"Yes, as are all my crew, and the crews of my other two ships," he replied with what I saw was great regret. Then I knew that he and his crews had been impressed into fighting for Doom against their will. They did it for survival only.

"Then you have no true loyalty to Lord Karlath Doom?"

"Loyalty to Lord Doom? No, none at all, Jon Kirk. We fear him, we even hate him, but we are not loyal to him beyond what we must do to survive, and have our families survive, so we have served him as we must do," the enemy captain told me. "We place ourselves under your control now. We are your prisoners. You could have us all killed now, such would be Lord Doom's order were your situation reversed."

"Yes, that would certainly be true, but I am not Lord Doom, nor anything like him, captain," I stated firmly, then I nodded and gave him a grim smile. I waited for his reply as he seemed to be thinking this new turn of events through to his best advantage.

"I see that now, or we would already be dead." the captain replied with a brief simple nod of his head. Waiting. Wondering what was to come next.

"Indeed. So tell me, what is your name, captain?" I asked the enemy commander.

"I am called Akar, captain of this warship, *The Attara*, which means *The Destructor*, in your language."

I nodded. "You and your crew gave a good account of yourselves, and I honor that warrior spirit, but I have an important question to ask you now. Would you and the crews of your three ships consider leaving your *consignat* status and becoming free people once again who will serve in our fleet?" I asked him, looking at him carefully for any signs of guile or deception. I saw none.

"You would do such a thing, offer such mercy to a defeated enemy? You would offer trust to an enemy?"

"No mercy, and no trust, to any enemy," I said firmly, them gave him a slight grin, "but to a friend, Captain Akar, to a friend, mercy and even trust is the least I can offer. Are you and the members of your crews interested in such an offer?"

"Yes! Of course, yes, we are, my… My Emperor, Jon Kirk."

"Then it is done," I told him simply. "Now that that is settled, Captain Akar, tell me, what was your mission in coming here to Ares, and what is Lord Doom's plan?'

Captain Akar shook his big wooly head in despair, "Truly, I am not sure, Jon Kirk. I was given orders to take my ship and these two other vessels and to make an attack upon Ares. I assumed we would be confronted before we ever got close to the planet. That is what happened. I do not know anything of the plan other than that. I assume it was an attempt to test the planetary projectile defenses—they are said to be considerable—or to draw away your feel. Which I did not think you would fall for. Or some manner of suicide plan he wanted to test using my ships and my crews. I do not know for certain, as Lord Doom does not confide his plans to me."

I nodded, it made sense. "Anything you can tell me that can help me defeat Doom, or understand his plans?"

The former enemy captain shrugged, opened his hands in help-lessness, "Not much, I am afraid. I know that Lord Doom nurtures a powerful hatred for you, Jon Kirk. It is truly awesome and terrible. It is said that it may even cloud his judgment in his service to the Master he serves. Lord Doom seeks your utter destruction at all costs."

I nodded, that did not faze me. "Even as I seek his destruction, captain."

"Then this is not the end of it, Jon Kirk?" Captain Akar asked in a soft tone.

"No, I am afraid it is just the beginning. Captain Kevnar have our warships reform and head back to Ares. Captain Akar, you and your two ships will follow us. You are now part of the Ares fleet. You now take your orders from Fleet Admiral Quarto-Zar—who takes his orders from me. Do you understand?"

"Yes, Jon Kirk, you are my emperor now, and I thank you for your mercy and trust to me and my crews—and for freeing us all from the control of Lord Doom."

And while Captain Akar and his crews were now free of Lord Doom, neither I nor Ares, could boast anything near as much. In fact, we seemed t be locked in a deadly death struggle that might bring us all down.

CHAPTER 2

A New Beginning

The room was dark and quiet. I sat in it alone, pondering all that had gone before and what was to come since I had first come to my new home world of the planet Ares so long ago now—an alien world 150 light years from Earth, far off in the Orion System.

I am Jon Kirk, former sergeant in the United States Army, who had been killed—and *not* killed—in a war in the jungles of Vietnam in 1968 during the Tet Offensive. I was dead—and not dead. I was a man who had mysteriously been transported to the far away planet Ares which now had become my home. It was all done by wily old Tar-gool's ancient transportation machine—a super-science device left over from the venerable Ancients of Ares. I now lived on a new and alien world, and yet it was one that I loved as much as my home world of Earth. I was a soldier, a fighter, a warrior who now lived and ruled under the glowing red sun that shone so brightly overhead, a blazing red sun that was called 'the fire in the sky', by the warlike people of Ares.

On Ares, a savage planet of endless battles and violence, I had found a home, a wife and won an empire. I had freed the green people—the Greens—from the hated monstrous tyranny of the evil Winged-men of Zar. I had fought and beaten the despot Okvon and his invisible blue men of Vognar—the Blues—from the land on the other side of the planet. I had caused the defeat of the war fleet of the Secret Empire of the Hundred Worlds, ruled by the mysterious and brutal Sindalki mind lords.

And yet, none of it seemed to be enough now.

Lord Karlath Doom, a demon prince of unimaginable mental powers and the worst of the Sindalki mind lords, still lived and had now become my greatest nemesis—though I had killed him in single combat in the very audience chamber of my palace here in Tarcos where I was seated now. All that had happened just a few days before.

I had killed Lord Doom in personal battle, and yet he would not die. For it was moments after his death—which had taken place right in front of so many of my people—when he had somehow regenerated. He had simply used some arcane Sindalki powers to bring himself back to life. He came back to life apparently unharmed at all by my deadly sword cuts, undamaged by the deep thrusts from my sharp blade, which had cut open his vitals. His wounds had been terrible, the damage fatal, yet he had healed before our eyes. Some form of instantaneous regeneration? I had no idea about the mystical Sindalki powers—but they were surely vast.

It was inconceivable. Lord Doom had died right in front of me, a death witnessed by a room full of my people, the leaders and ministers of the empire I now ruled, but he soon came back to life as we watched in abject terror. It was amazing and horrifying. Once he had come back to life we were shocked to see that there was suddenly no longer even one wound upon him and he merely laughed at me as he promised his most dire revenge upon me and my family.

I did not doubt his threats for one second.

Then he simply disappeared.

* * * *

I wondered where Doom had gone to and what he was up to.

Lord Karlath Doom was a Sindalki nobleman and as such had many mysterious mind powers—the dark powers possessed by the Sindalki lords—of which all of his race were now dead and gone. This had been accomplished compliments of Lord Doom himself. Lord Doom had simply exterminated his own people, which I assumed had been done in an effort to eliminate his competition. He had used the powers of his Enemy Empire fleet of a hundred warships to destroy his own home world. It was inconceivable and showed the depth of his treachery, betrayal and depravity.

Now the Sindalki race was no more—their planet and race were all gone and dead—except for one poor lonely wretch, Lord Kneth—who had been taken for healing by Aron the Eldest, and the other sages of Kev, to their mysterious secret city located somewhere upon Ares. Lord Kneth had witnessed the great betrayal of his empire and his people by Lord Doom—something that his psyche could not accept as ever being possible. He could not conceive of such treachery. However, it *was* possible—for it had all happened. The reality of what had been done, the vast deep treason that had caused the murder of all his people and his world, had shaken this last Sindalki lord to the very core of his soul. Lord Kneth was now a shell of the man he had once been, and he was now severely ill.

Meanwhile, my deadly nemesis, Lord Karlath Doom lived on and now controlled the vast fleet of the Enemy Empire, as well as all the creatures who followed the unknown alien entity called the Kin-Ty-Roo—or by some, known as The Being Who is Not To Be Named. What powers this strange alien being possessed were unknown, but for a monster like Doom to become one of its most feared and devoted minions, meant that the alien entity had to be a creature of inconceivable power and evil darkness. It was thought to be extremely dangerous and deeply malevolent. More malevolent even than the Secret Empire that had been controlled by the Sindalki lords—where the world of Sindalki was no more. The planet had been destroyed and all on it vaporized. Doom had caused that genocide to cement his own power. And now Doom was still free and up to some terrible treachery that I knew he would turn against Ares and myself.

If only I could figure out what he planned and stop it before he put it into operation.

I had recently, and most reluctantly, been proclaimed Emperor of the Greens of my world, and Emperor of all Ares, and I had been further forced to accept the title of Emperor of our area of Orion space, what is termed the Known Universe. It was all quite a mouthful for me to accept and I was the first to laugh at the absurd idea of it all— had it not been so deadly serious. I had been forced to reluctantly take on the duty of emperor—for there had been no other serious choice. It had been made quite clear to me by all the leaders, that I was the only one who could unite and hold together the disparate races of Ares, and all the various planetary worlds of what had once been the Secret Empire of the Hundred Worlds. I was the only one who could hold them together into a free and fair union of disparate worlds—a new empire—a *better* empire! It was now my duty to rule them all in this new empire that was united to fight and defeat Lord

Karlath Doom—and eventually the dark entity that controlled him, the deadly mysterious alien entity known as the Kin-Ty-Roo.

I thought of the super weapons we now had at our disposal, the powerful killing death rays, the mask of invisibility—but I shook my head sadly when I considered them now. None of them would help us in this new war. Our enemy had the same death rays, and the same shields to negate those weapons, and they also had the ability to make their soldiers and ships invisible. Both sides in this war had the ability to use invisibility—and both sides could also negate and see through the mirage of invisibility. So our power of invisibility that had been of such great help to us in past battles upon Ares, was of no use to us any longer in this great space war we found ourselves engaged in. This was a new war, with new rules, and it was most distressing to realize this. I feared we were unprepared for what we were to go up against. I knew I was unprepared for what was to come, but I was determined to meet it and defeat it—whatever it might be.

These grim thoughts were interrupted when I heard loud purposeful steps coming near my rooms from the outer hall, and then there was a quick knocking upon the door to my chamber. It was Zaor, my good friend, brother-in-law, and the man I had made our First General. He entered my rooms. I looked over at him with a slight smile that could not quite hide my growing despair.

"Why the grim face, Jon Kirk?" he spoke up in his usual jaunty manner.

"I fear I have taken on more than I can handle," I told my friend, the brother of my wife, Sirah. "I fear we can not win going up against such insurmountable odds."

"You have done nothing but win against insurmountable odds since you first came here to Ares, Jon Kirk—since my sister, Sirah, my wife, Manalia, and I first saw you upon our world. You have accomplished much, caused many great victories, My Emperor. I am sure you can do anything."

"Not anything. I fear this time our challenges may be impossible to overcome."

"For you, the impossible just takes a little longer," Zaor responded with a wide grin, showing a firm faith in me that I myself did not feel.

I shook my head with a wan smile, "Well, that is certainly good to hear, but we need to act right away on this in the correct manner. We need to get the fleet together, all the spaceships that Admiral Quarto of Zar has taken control of from the former Secret Empire war fleet. We have just added three more warships and crews, by the way. Then we need to track down Lord Doom and destroy him."

"That is true," Zaor replied in a sharp tone. "We would all like to see that done. Does the commander of the newly captured ships know anything that can help us?"

"Hah, not much I am afraid, his mind has been blocked and he has been kept to very limited knowledge. We can expect no help from him to find Lord Doom, though none would like to find him more than I. But where do we find him?" I asked, for I was wracked by doubt about what our next course of action should be. For I knew that if I moved the fleet away from Ares in one direction, it would leave other worlds of the empire open to attack. If I took the fleet away from its post orbiting Ares, my own home world would also be left under defended. Even with the use of the massive platform death ray projectors set atop the mountains of this world, they were not as powerful as the weapons of the entire fleet. My wife, Sirah, my son, Alun, and all the Greens and Blues of Ares would be without our most potent defense if I moved the fleet away. I did not want to do that. So what to do?

"You still live, Jon Kirk," Zaor told me showing a wry grin, speaking back to me the bold words that was the warrior motto I often employed in my darkest moments. These were the true words of the fighting man everywhere.

"Yes, I still live—*we* still live," I said with a grim smile.

"That is something, is it not?"

"Yes, my friend, that certainly is something. In fact, it is very much indeed," I admitted in a low tone.

When you consider all that we had gone through we had certainly beaten the odds, but my mind was whirling with questions and plans, theories and suppositions. The future seemed all too confusing and full of unknowns. There was not enough data about our enemy—not enough was known for me to make any definitive plan of attack or defense. I feared we were being stymied by the power of this Kin-

Ty-Roo. I spoke up firmly, "We need more information, we need intelligence on Doom's plans."

"So then we must obtain it?" Zaor told me simply. "In the meantime we must try to find out his next move. Though it is easier said than done."

"Yes, but we must also prepare. Actually *you* must prepare for war. I want you to call in all the leaders of every world united with us, send the call out to every world loyal to our new empire and have them make ready their warships, and prepare their warriors for a great battle to come."

"Yes, My Emperor, I will prepare all," Zaor told me eagerly, his warrior spirit excited by the prospect of impending action, "but in the meantime, may I ask, what will you be doing?"

"I am taking another trip, via Tar-gool's machine, back to the Earth. I need to be sure of events there that I have a great fear about."

"Doom?" Zaor asked me quietly.

I nodded. "I need to be assured of something that I fear may happen there and once I am sure it is safe, I shall then go to the secret city of Kev and seek out Aron the Eldest and Lord Kneth, for there are answers these wise old men can give me that I am sure they have kept locked in their hearts and minds for a thousand years. Now is the time for them to join us and not hold back on any of their knowledge or powers."

"The mind masters scare me, Jon Kirk. They hold many dark and dangerous secrets, I fear." Zaor sat softly.

"I am sure they do," I replied thoughtfully.

CHAPTER 3

My Visit To Earth

My visit to Earth this time was not one of pleasure or fun, it was not to merely visit my old friend from the days of youth, as the previous trips had been. This time it was for a reason that was quite different. While my physical body was comfortably seated in the couch of Tar-gool's machine back home in my palace in Tarcos on Ares—the image and form of my body was being instantaneously transported 150 light years to the Earth, the third planet in the Sol System.

Pinpoint targeting by the ancient machine deposited me gently in the street of my old friend's neighborhood in his city upon the Earth, in my nation of the United States of America. I looked around at the quaint homes of the suburban neighborhood and smiled as I walked. All appeared as it had always been. I breathed the cool brisk air, it filled my lungs. I looked around at the small but lovely little homes and some of the local people. All seemed to be healthy. All seemed to be safe. It was most enjoyable for me to see this once again. All seemed to be in its proper place. That was certainly reassuring to me, for I was full of great trepidation just then.

I slowly strode up the red brick walkway to my old friend's house, right up to his front door. I rang the bell. There was no answer. I rang it again. Finally I heard some commotion from inside the home, heavy footsteps pounding down stairs. Suddenly the front door was flung open and my old friend stood there framed in the doorway. It was good to see him. He was surely a sight for sore eyes. He had aged a bit, but his image was unmistakable to me—as I am sure my image was to him. He looked at me with surprise, shock, and then, I was relieved to see, absolute joy break out upon his big smiling face.

"Jon? Jon Kirk, is it truly you?"

"Who else, my friend," I replied returning his warm smile. "I have returned from Ares to see how you are, and how Earth is doing these days. May I come in?"

"Yes, yes, of course! Please come in," he replied and led me into his home, through a short hall and then into a modest living room where he brought me over to a large soft chair to sit down upon. I sat and relaxed.

"Can I offer you something? Anything? A drink?"

I smiled. "It may be too early for a beer, but in any case you know that this image is merely a projection, and while it has form and substance to it, it is not really the actual physical me," I reminded him.

"Yes, of course, this is the work of Tar-gool's machine as you once told me."

"That is true. Tar-gool's machine, but I have since learned he did not create the machine, but rescued it from the Ancients of Ares, who created it with their super-science thousands of years ago."

"Super-science?" he said in awe. "Thousands of years ago? That sounds like they are far ahead of us here on Earth?

"They *were*, but that is a tale for another day. There are many strange things that I have come here to tell you concerning my life and travels upon Ares, but there are things that I must know from you as well now."

"What are they, Jon?" he responded, a bit surprised by my request. "Of course I will be glad to help you with anything that I am able."

"Good. So tell me, what is happening these days on Earth? The wars, the political situation between nations? How is the United States faring these days?"

"You mean since you left?"

"Yes, I guess that would be the best place to start," I asked him.

"Well, politics and history was always a hobby of mine, as you know. So I do pay attention to the news and history. Well, first of all, since you fought—and died there in Vietnam—but did not die—I guess you should know that we won in Vietnam. What I mean to say is that militarily, we were victorious. However, we lost the war through…well it was through the betrayal and incompetence of politics."

"It is ever the way," I admitted softly, this was sad news to hear but not unexpected. The fighting men secure the victory with their blood and the politicians throw it away as if it is something they never, ever wanted at all. Or they sell it! For profit, or votes. Political expediency. I tamped down my anger. That was all in the past. I was concerned about the present, and the future now.

My friend only nodded, then further explained. "Today it is many years later and there are new threats, new enemies, but our country is strong if it can only be united behind a good leader. We have had too many of the bad or weak kind lately—and sometimes even worse—corrupt and evil. It is ever the way. But the American people are strong and brave. The people are fearless and remain free."

I nodded; that was good to hear. "They sound like the people of Ares."

"I am sure that people are people everywhere, Jon."

"Yes, I am sure you are right."

"But what exactly is it you are after? For I detect something is bothering you. Is it that bit regarding the Secret Empire you told me about on your last visit? I remember what you had said, and I tell you now that it has bothered me quite a bit."

"Yes, since then there has been much trouble. The home world of the Sindalki has been destroyed and the Sindalki race has been exterminated, millions were killed, excepting only two individuals who remain of all that vast race of people."

"An entire race killed? An entire planet destroyed?"

"Yes," I responded quietly.

"But that's genocide—genocide on a massive—on a planetary scale!"

"Yes it is, and... Well, I have come here..."

"Why exactly have you come here, Jon?"

"Well, I..."

"Do you fear for the Earth?" he asked carefully. My friend was a most perceptive individual.

"Yes I do, and while I did not want to alarm you, I truly feared what I might find here when Tar-gool's old machine projected my body to the Earth. However I am much relieved to discover that you are all well and alive and everything is apparently normal here on Earth."

"Or as normal as it can be," my friend responded with a mild laugh, trying to hide his tension and concern. I could see the fear growing in his eyes now.

I allowed a slim smile, "Yes, or as normal as things can be on Earth, my old friend. So I am glad to see that so far nothing has been done to disturb the Earth. But tell me, have you heard any strange stories, perhaps of aliens, spaceships—UFOs we used to call them. Have you heard anything like that in the news lately?"

"No, nothing but the usual. There are always some silly stories in the news but they turn out to be nothing. However, I think I understand what you are asking. I think you are asking me if anything has happened significant, like in that old Michael Rennie science fiction film we saw as kids, *The Day the Earth Stood Still*. Remember that? So no, we have not been visited by any alien beings, nor any embassy from another planet. No alien spaceship has landed in the Mall in Washington D.C., or in Central Park in New York City."

I allowed a brief sigh in relief. If Doom was here, he would have surely made his presence known in some spectacular way.

"I have to tell you that a Sindalki mind master by the name of Lord Karlath Doom is loose and I am sure he is up to no good. We have no idea where he is now or what he is up to, but he is extremely dangerous. I am just thankful that he is apparently not here on Earth causing trouble."

My friend nodded. "No, nothing like that has happened, Jon."

I sighed. "Well, that is good."

As is always the way, I had spoken too soon.

Suddenly, as if on cue—in fact as if he had been watching us all along listening to our conversation—a bright shimmering light filled my friend's living room and a moment later the fearsome image of Lord Karlath Doom boldly stood there in front of me and my friend. We were both astonished by the sudden appearance of the bright flashing image—but for different reasons.

My friend stood up and shouted boldly at our uninvited visitor, "Who are you? What the hell is this?"

I knew we were beyond the use of words now.

Lord Doom ignored him but smiled wickedly at me, a terrible death head's grin of blackest hatred and evil. He then looked around him at the room and its contents, "How utterly primitive. Oh well, soon it shall be no more. This is your doing, Jon Kirk, your paltry home world. I promised you utter defeat and destruction once I attained the power of all of the Sindalki, and now through the added strength supplied through the Kin-Ty-Roo, I have become invulnerable. All that has now come to pass, and now it is your turn to taste my revenge."

I knew the image was a mere projection, as was my own image, so there was no way to fight against him. I looked at it quickly trying to come up with some plan of action, and then as suddenly as it had appeared, the image of Doom vanished completely.

He was gone.

One moment Lord Doom was there—then he was not. I wondered why. What was he up to?

"What the hell was that about, Jon? What revenge did hemean? Who is he and where did he go? Where the hell did he come from anyway?" my friend asked me in astonished fear now. "Who is he, Jon?"

"That is him—or his image—Lord Karlath Doom. He is here now. Somewhere here on Earth, or on a warship out in planetary orbit. I am sorry," I said in a grim whisper.

"Sorry? Why are you sorry, Jon?"

"Because his being here now means that…"

I never was able to complete the next word in that sentence.

The room around us instantly began to spin and swirl and then explode into a whirlwind of bright light and painfully loud sounds. The walls of the house, the entire neighborhood seemed to just melt away as I watched in awe and rage at the utter destruction that was taking place. My own transported image was unaffected by the chaos and damage swirling all around me since I was just a mere projection, but everything else was exploding and melting away everywhere as I watched in abject horror. People screamed. People were dying. Then there was a deadly quiet. Soon everything was gone. It had all been destroyed. I could not believe what had just happened—what I had just witnessed!

My body floated there alone, now surrounded by a swirling mass of utter destruction and chaos. Rock and debris swirled around me like I was within the eye of some monstrous hurricane. I feared what this might mean. Though I did not want to accept what I had now seen happen with my very own eyes, in my heart I knew what it meant.

I knew now that the planet Earth no longer existed.

Then I had a sudden disoriented dizzy feeling and felt myself falling.

What was happening now?

It was Tar-gool's machine kicking into emergency mode, and it had immediately pulled my projection back to Ares. My thoughts and memories of what I had just seen, my image and perceptions now crossed the void of space and I was brought back home to Ares. I awoke startled from my dream travel through space, my eyes full of tears, my mind numb and shaken by what I had just witnessed. Had it been real? I did not want to believe that it could be true, but I knew that it was true. I had seen it all with my own eyes.

Earth was no more!

The Earth had been destroyed by Lord Karlath Doom. Billions of innocent people were now dead, exterminated! Another planetary genocide. I cried, as my fist pounded the arm rest of the couch that held my actual physical body in impotent rage and pain. Ras-noor's assistants ran over, helped me out of the device and asked what was wrong.

"Has the machine malfunctioned in some way?" I remember hearing one of the technicians ask me through my mental haze and anguish. I could not reply. How could I even speak of what I had just seen done? An entire world had been destroyed before my very eyes!

I said nothing. I was in total shock. I could not even scream in rage or cry in pain yet. Earth was gone. Destroyed. How could it be?

The Earth was no more!

CHAPTER 4

Aftermath

Earth, my home world, along with the billions of people who lived there—it was all gone now—the result of one short horrible cataclysmic event. It had only taken one moment to accomplish total destruction. An infinitesimally powerful attack of devastating power had done it. I knew what I had witnessed was true. I felt it painfully within my heart, within my very soul. The lovely home world of my birth had been blown out of existence by Lord Karlath Doom's warship and his terrible super-weapons.

Earth never had a chance!

I had thought—I had hoped—that my seeing Doom's projection appear in my friend's living room might mean that it had been sent from a ship far away—maybe somewhere far beyond Ares, or elsewhere far away in the depths of the Known Universe. I never thought his image was being projected directly from a lone Enemy Empire warship that was then in Earth orbit. Certainly not from a ship ready to destroy my home world. I found myself utterly numb from the realization of what had transpired. How could he—*even a monster such as Doom*—do such a terrible thing? Destroy an entire world, and all the billions who lived upon it! But I knew Doom was the worst kind of depraved villain. He had, after all, murdered his own entire race, destroyed his own home world of Sindalki—so it seemed nothing was beyond Doom's sheer destructive madness.

"What is it, my beloved?" I heard the sweet voice of my wife, and empress, Sirah ask of me as she cradled my shaking body in her arms. Her voice grew more frantic, as she shouted out to attendants, "Bring me blankets! Bring drink! What has happened, Jon?"

I had not noticed she had even entered the room.

"Earth…" I muttered, shaking, trembling.

"Yes?" she asked curiously, for she knew that I occasionally used Tar-gool's machine to travel back to visit my home world to see old friends.

I whispered in a cold rasping voice, "It—it is gone!"

She looked at me with wide-eyed terror and shock, instantly comprehending the horror of it all. For she knew Lord Doom as well as I did, and what he was capable of.

There was nothing else that could be said. She understood only too well knowing Lord Doom and the mind powers and super scientific forces available to the Sindalki—and the threat it also meant to Ares and our own people now.

"I am so sorry," she whispered softly, holding me tightly in her arms. I thanked God for her love more than ever at that moment, for I needed it more than ever.

"Sorry? Yes, so am I. I suspected—but I never prepared for this. I never actually thought he would do such a terrible thing—that anyone could ever do such a thing!" I rasped broken words wracked with great emotional pain, and a profound guilt, then I broke down into tears as she, and her brother, Zaor, tried their best to comfort me. I cried for the destroyed Earth and all that was lost now. Then a new thought grabbed me—for now I also feared for my beloved Ares, and all that might be lost here very soon. What was I to do now? What could I do?

It was the most difficult situation I had ever been in during my entire life on Earth, or upon Ares. It was the end of the planet of my birth, the end of all the people I knew—and billions I did not know. Lives snuffed out without a thought, without even the realization that the end for them had come. Their useless deaths struck me to the very core of my being. I was seriously fearful that my mind might crack and break under the realization of what I had seen done to the Earth. Images of the planet exploding and melting before my eyes lingered in my mind. Images of people…it was horrendous! Lord Doom, no doubt, wished this reaction from me, hence his visit to me on Earth to issue his threat. He had obviously been watching and waiting for me to arrive before he had done his deadly deed so that I could view it all. He had surely enjoyed causing such destruction and inflicting such pain and suffering upon my world—and on myself.

I now felt that I fully understood the great distress and melancholy that had overtaken Lord Kneth after Doom had destroyed the Sindalki home world and murdered the entire Sindalki race. I could feel nothing but heartbroken sadness for that last Sindalki lord who was now being treated by Aron the Eldest, and the other mind masters in far off Kev. I realized also now that the mind masters were the answer to all that was transpiring. Their great mental powers might be able to reach that dark place in Lord Kneth and save him, or at least help him. With his restoration to sanity, and with Lord Kneth's help, I might be able to bring down Lord Doom. For I realized that I needed Lord Kneth and his Sindalki knowledge in the coming battle with Doom. I also needed some of that help now for myself. I hoped that same aid might be given to me—for I was not ready to fight another battle just yet, but I was not ready to give up either. I would never give up!

I had now become the last and only Earthman left alive in the Known Universe—but I was not going to accept that fate, and I was not going down to defeat without a fight. I was not going to go gently into that good night. I would do all I could to triumph! I had no choice. It is the will of the true warrior. The code of the fighting man is to never give up. I had to find a way to defeat Doom and in doing so I could at least save my beloved Sirah, my son, my people, and my new home world of Ares.

I still lived! And with those three simple words I realized I was now more determined than ever to achieve victory—and destroy Lord Doom. I would follow him to the end of the Known Universe or beyond to achieve that end!

I looked to my friend and general, Zaor.

"Convene the War Council, we are to make ready for battle," I said with a firm tone now, grasping my fragile emotions and holding them in check by sheer will power. And anger, and rage and even hatred helped. For I pledged that Lord Karlath Doom was going to pay for what he had done to the Earth and all the innocent people who had once lived there. He would be made to pay if it was the last thing I ever did!

* * * *

"Quiet down! Quiet down, I say! The Emperor is here!" It was the large burly Viking-like alien named Gorm of the Gorms whose powerful voice now rang resoundingly throughout the huge audience chamber of the Imperial Palace at Tarcos. "The Emperor comes! All hail, Jon Kirk, Emperor of the Greens and Blues, Emperor of Ares, Emperor of the Known Universe!"

There were instant cheers and cries of joy, but I hardly noticed them at all. Even Gorm's overly dramatic announcement of my so-called august imperial presence did not annoy me this day as it usually did. I paid it no mind. This day was for business—serious business of war and revenge.

I walked over to the seat I used that was strategically placed at the front of the huge room. Some would call it a throne—even an imperial throne—but to me it was just a big fancy chair. Not even very comfortable. I sat down and looked over at all the people in that room full of ministers, military leaders, planetary governors, advisors and others who with me ruled the former worlds of the Secret Empire of the Sindalki's. Some were present through image projections, others on screens through video imaging. All looked to me now to lead them, they nodded, or saluted, and gave me their undivided attention.

"Thank you all for being here on such short notice, my friends," I told them, reaching in my mind for the words that I needed to tell them. It was difficult. While some there said I was a natural leader, I did not feel like one, and I was certainly no politician or diplomat. I looked over at the faces in that crowd and spoke up in a strong bold voice, so each one there could not only hear my words, but they could feel my words, "My friends, we are at war. Though the Secret Empire of the Sindalki lords is no more, our war is not yet done nor won—though we are now all that remains of that dead empire. We are all now part of a new better empire of united worlds that I seem to have most reluctantly inherited as your leader. So be it!"

I paused for a moment and there was a low murmur and a few conciliatory nods of various wise heads. Then I continued, "But let us not forget, we are still at war with this so-called other empire, known as the Enemy Empire. That means war against the master of that empire, the alien entity known as the Kin-Ty-Roo, and his minion, Lord Karlath Doom, the traitorous Sindalki lord. Many of you have heard the news by now of what Lord Doom has done to his own

Sindalki home world, and also to my own home world of the Earth. Over 150 light years from Ares, Doom took his flagship and used it to destroy the planet of my birth. Earth. The planet had no defenses against his super weapons. We now know that Earth was exploded into a billion billion pieces. There were no survivors. I am the last Earthman."

There were murmurs of great sadness and regret among those present. And rumblings of impending fear.

Ras-noor, my chief scientist suddenly spoke up, "There has been a massive violent change noted in the Sol System."

I nodded sadly, "The Sol System now has *two* asteroid belts; the previous one being between the planets of Mars and Jupiter; and now a newer and more unstable one between the planets Venus and Mars—where the Earth had once been."

There was total quite throughout the huge chamber now. Astonishment. Dread.

I halted for another sad moment, collected my thoughts, then began with renewed purpose and a strong defiant voice, "I mourn the loss of many billions of my people, even as Lord Kneth of Sindalki mourns the loss of his home world and his own people. This massive death and destruction on a planetary scale must stop. We must work together to put an end to Lord Doom and the empire of this entity known as the Kin-Ty-Roo that he serves. We must do this soon, before they come for us to destroy our people and our worlds. And they will be coming for us soon! Make no mistake about that!"

I paused, allowing everyone there enough time to digest my words. I knew they were heard as fearful and terrifying words. I saw shock and fear upon many faces. I expected no less, for it was terrible news that I had to give them this day.

"My friends, we must fight and we must win!" I continued firmly, showing them all much more confidence than I truly felt. Then I steeled myself for the orders I had to give. I knew they would go hard with many of the representatives there, but it had to be done this way. Ares had to be protected at all cost. That was because I knew this planet was the next target of Doom's wrath, now that he had destroyed the Earth. Ares would be next.

"First off, we must protect our headquarters world, and that means that I will order Admiral Quarto-Zar to keep our fleet in orbit around Ares to protect this world and its people for the present. Thus we will protect our government and leadership, our scientific leaders, and our mind masters, and it will give us a safe base to plan our attack. The death ray projector platforms placed upon the mountain tops of this world will also offer it further protection from enemy warships. I have also ordered Ras-noor and his teams to build even larger and more powerful weapons for us to use to protect this world. Soon these death ray projector platforms will be sent and set up on many of your own home worlds—the worlds of the Gorms, the Tergats, to Caxtar and Talu, to Ko-Ah-Leh, and even the planet Zar and the world of the Blue Kortas. All your home worlds will soon be protected as much as possible. You will not be forgotten. You are not alone."

There were some cheers at these words, but I could see some in that chamber wondered why they should not be sent the miracle weapons immediately—why did they have to wait? Or why must the fleet stay back and protect only Ares? I knew I had to answer those important questions now.

"There is a reason for all this and you all deserve answers, so here they are. It is hard truth, so it is a bitter pill we must all swallow. Ares must be protected at all costs. Ares, as the capitol of our new empire, will certainly be the next target of Lord Doom's wrath and he must not succeed, for he seeks to destroy this world, as he did the Earth and his own Sindalki home world. Your own home worlds are safe for now—until after he takes out his will upon Ares. He is coming here first. So we must stop him here! That is why the fleet must stay posted here—and with our death ray platform projectors on this planet—we will make it difficult—if not impossible for his fleet to conquer this world. Or for him to destroy it as he has done to other worlds. We can make our stand here! We can stop him here! But it may be only for a short while. We can stop him for a time—slow down his attack—delay his victory—but we need to do more than that. We need to utterly defeat him! Once and for all. There must be no substitute for victory!"

There were a few cheers but there was also quiet by too many throughout the chamber. Everyone there digesting my words, wondering what we were to do. All wondering how we were to defeat Lord Doom and attain this glorious victory. None more so than I.

"Can we divide the fleet, sending some warships to each of the member worlds of our empire? At least that would offer these worlds some protection," one of the outer world representatives spoke the question upon many minds there.

"If we divide the fleet, that will mean its destruction," I said simply.

"I agree, or it would make our fleet totally ineffective," Admiral Quarto-Zar spoke up in a loud voice, and that was all that seemed to be need said upon that question.

There was some light mumbling and consternation among the throng at these words, though they now seemed to accept them.

"The Admiral has spoken!" Gorm of the Gorms growled meaningfully. He looked around at the throng, waiting, hoping for anyone to defy him. There were no more questions. That closed down the discussion on that topic.

I nodded, stood up, looked into the faces of each of those powerful men and women. "Rest assured your home worlds are safe for now. Ares will certainly be Doom's next target. He is coming for this world even now. I have no way to know how he will attack us, or what forces he will use, but he has a vast fleet of Kin-Ty-Roo warships so it will probably be another massive battle set in orbit around this world like our last fight. We won that battle. I know not what is coming. In the meantime, get your warships and your worlds ready to defend themselves and fight. We know not what threat we will face in the future but I tell you all this—I make you this promise—we will be victorious! I will take my revenge upon Lord Doom for all the evil he has done, and then this Kin-Ty-Roo will taste bloody painful defeat!"

There were cheers aplenty now at my inspiring and bold words. They had been said with utter confidence, a confidence that I did not truly feel, but a confidence that I did truly believe within my heart. A warrior's heart that was full of fire and fury.

I nodded at all the leaders who were there from all over Ares, and others from over a dozen other worlds, all my friends, advisors and ministers. They trusted me, they had accepted my promise of victory. That was gratifying. Now I only hoped that I would be able to keep my promise.

* * * *

I called Sahn-Jor, Zaor, and my wife, Sirah, into a small private room off the main audience chamber. These were the three people who I most trusted in my life. They were all totally loyal to me. Sahn-Jor, my most able minister and friend; Zaor, my best friend and greatest warrior general; and my beloved Sirah, my wife and empress, who was so wise and loving. The most important and closest people to me in my life—other than my young son, Alun. Alun was still a child then, but growing up fast. I looked over at the man who was my First Minister.

"Sahn-Jor, I am going away for a while," I informed him.

"Jon!" Sirah asked me showing her surprise, for I had not spoken of this plan with her beforehand as I usually would do.

I held her tightly and kissed her glossy green lips as I brushed back her shimmering green hair. "My love, I must go, there are important things I need to learn. Earth was destroyed for a reason. I can not believe it was only because of Doom's revenge and hatred against me. There must be more to it than that. I am going to seek out Aron the Eldest and his people. I need to get them onboard with our coming fight. I must learn all they know in order to enlist their support before I can proceed with this war against Doom and the alien entity he serves."

"What exactly do these ancients know, Jon Kirk?" Zaor asked me curiously.

"I am not sure, my friend. I do not know, but I feel they hold many secrets and have many unknown powers. I need to know what they know and to convince them to join us, and to willingly fight with us."

Sahn-jor told me plainly, "They will not help us, Jon Kirk. They are a most isolated people and fervently wish to remain so."

"I know that, but I will somehow get them to join our cause," I replied firmly.

"That may be impossible," Sahn-jor told me in a soft tone. I had sent him many months back to try to find the secret city of the mind masters of Kev and he had not been able to do so.

Zaor shook his head with disagreement, "It is a bad time for you to leave here when we might be under attack at any moment."

"You are correct, my friend, but I must do it. Ares should be safe for now. I do not believe Ares will be under attack at this moment, nor in the immediate future. Doom is planning something. Something special. I believe that it is taking him some time to put his plan into operation. I believe that means there is still time yet for us to remain safe before he acts. I will be quick, but I must leave and seek out the mind masters of Kev. I need to find answers."

"I hope you find the answers you seek, Jon Kirk," Sahn-Jor stated with a warm but sad smile.

"I do too. I want you to run the everyday business of the empire, Sahn-Jor. There is no one I trust more with this duty than you. And you, Zaor, my brother in fighting spirit and family blood, I want you to lead our army and fleet if the time comes that I do not return."

"I will do so, My Emperor, but I know you will be here to lead us yourself when you do return," Zaor said confidently.

I smiled at his loyalty. It was truly touching.

"And you, my beloved Sirah, keep our little Alun safe, and I will be back before the attack on Ares."

"My husband, I know not why you are going on this mission at this time, nor can I understand it, but if you believe it to be important, then it must be important. I pray you keep safe, come back home to me soon," she said softly. I could see that she was bravely holding back tears.

"I will do my best," was the only reply I could give her.

She smiled at that, "Then that is enough for me, Jon Kirk. For your best is as good to me as any guarantee of victory. So I shall fear no more."

"Fear no more," I said, speaking the old Ares warrior phrase that had become a code to many fighting men of my adopted world.

"Fear no more," she whispered as I left her.

CHAPTER 5

Out of Tarcos

I took one man with me on my desperate journey out of Tarcos to find the secret city of Kev, which was hidden somewhere upon the vast and wild planet of Ares. That man was the bold young warrior, Tor-nul, captain of the Black Dragons, my Imperial Bodyguard. He would serve as a companion and messenger and an aid should I need one. He was a good warrior to have at your side in any dangerous undertaking, brave, loyal and a fellow with a very good sword arm.

"Where are we going, My Emperor?" the young officer asked me. It was obvious to me that he was proud that I had chosen him to accompany me upon this secret mission into unknown and dangerous territory.

"To the mysterious city of Kev, or whatever it is called. The city where Aron the Eldest and King Shamar, and what is left of the Keven people, now live. They are in hiding, so they will be hard to find. They do not seek interaction with the outside world. Sahn-Jor seems to believe they have founded a new underground and secret city on the western continent of the Vognars, the land of the Blues. So it shall be there where we are headed."

Tor-nul nodded his head accepting what I had said, which was all fine with him. "You need only ask of me what you want done and I shall do it, My Emperor, even if it should lead to the end of my own life."

I looked carefully at Tor-nul and shook my head negatively with a slight grin, "No, my friend, you are not to lose your life for me. I will have none of it, and while we are at it, stop calling me with that silly honorific 'my emperor'. I am just Jon Kirk. We are fellow warriors traveling together upon a simple quest, and that is all."

"Yes, My Emperor—I mean…Jon Kirk."

I laughed. "That is better, now let us be off."

Tor-nul, who had hated all things pertaining to flight not very long ago, had now since learned how to fly the smaller planetary fliers quite well so that he quietly and effortlessly guided our small vessel into the air, and soon we were smoothly climbing up into the crimson atmosphere of Ares. The mighty red sun above us shone with its usual bright red fire, the double moons visible even in the daylight stood out like two bright white pearls upon the horizon, as if great eyes looking down upon us from the depths of space. It was a lovely world and a stunning vision of burning crimson. A bright red world, a world of blood and battle, a planet of war, the world that I loved.

"Which direction, Jon Kirk?"

"Due west, to Vognar—and whatever awaits us there."

"Due west it is."

* * * *

The underground city of Kev was newly built and most secret, secure, undetectable. King Shamar was surprised when Aron the Eldest, and other members of the Elder Council, all of whom were powerful mind masters, came to see him in his audience chamber that morning. The Elders did not often interfere with the day to day operation of his tiny kingdom. Or with the king.

"Lord Aron, fellow Elders, it is good to see you all again," King Shamar said invitingly as the group of older green men approached their youthful warrior monarch. The people of Kev had remained independent for millennia, free of the torment of the Winged-men of Zar who had conquered Ares so long ago. They had lived free in a secret city on the eastern continent of Cos for many centuries, and did not overly concern themselves with the lives of other men—Green men, or the Greens. It was only when the blue men, or Blues from Vognar—from that mysterious unknown western continent who had allied themselves with the Winged-men to re-conquer the Green cities newly freed by the outworlder Jon Kirk—it was only then when the Kevens became involved in the great war. They flew the black ships that destroyed the Vognar fleet, but they lost their beloved city of Keva as a result.

After many battles and a final victory in the great war that finally won Ares independence, Lord Aron and King Shamar had proved instrumental in convincing Jon Kirk to take the throne he had been offered and to become the ruler of a new empire. So Jon Kirk became emperor—not only of the Greens on the eastern continent of Cos—and not only of all Ares—but now he had been proclaimed Emperor of all the worlds of the Known Universe. He was appointed leader of all the various races and planets, alien beings and alien worlds which had now united and unanimously appointed Jon Kirk as their leader—as their protector, benefactor—as emperor.

Aron the Eldest, wisest and oldest sage of the Kevens, along with King Shamar of Kev, knew all this recent history only too well. They had helped make it come to pass.

"Well, as I told you, he is on his way here," Aron told his king with a slight sigh. He had expected this, of course. Jon Kirk was no fool, and Aron knew as emperor he would seek out the answers to the many questions the events of recent history now posed. Many dire challenges lay ahead and the consequences for failure meant total destruction.

"But…why?" King Shamar asked the venerable sage curiously.

Lord Aron smiled indulgently at his youthful monarch, "For answers, that is why."

"What do we know that we can tell him? I mean, I know very little that I can tell him and I am king and know quite a lot—but you…? Ah, yes, wise old Aron, I know you have much secret knowledge. I feel you know much more that you do not ever speak of—even to me."

"That is true, my king."

Shamar was a bit surprised by that admission, but not overly so, for he had surmised as much for many years. Lord Aron and his group of mind masters possessed great mental powers that dwarfed even those of the young king and all others of Kev. They were now known as the mind masters and the name was certainly accurate, for they could accomplish such incredible actions with their minds that most of the people of Ares could never imagine possible.

The king asked, "Then you will help Jon Kirk and give him the answers that he seeks?"

"Yes, I feel that it is time we must do so. You see, his home world, the Earth, has recently been destroyed by Lord Doom. I fear Ares is next. Of course that places us in imminent danger as Ares is our world as well. Danger of extinction. However, that is not the worst of what we face, for this Lord Doom is but one evil minion of the feasting entity known as the Kin-Ty-Roo. The true enemy we all must ultimately battle. However, Lord Doom must be destroyed first, and then the master he serves must also be destroyed. We must help Jon Kirk achieve this aim. It is something that we and all the races of the Known Universe must join together to achieve, or we will all be destroyed. It is really quite simple now. We all face ultimate extinction. We must fight. We have no choice."

The king sighed deeply, his face grim and dark with concern at this terrible realization. This was a far worse situation than he had ever thought possible.

"But how can Jon Kirk accomplish this? He is but one lone man?" the king asked curiously. He knew the emperor well, and liked him, but as much of a fighter as he was, he knew Jon Kirk was after all, just one man—and an outworlder at that!

Lord Aron nodded thoughtfully.

King Shamar looked at him and continued. "This Kin-Ty-Roo seems all powerful from what I have been told. Is it not inevitable, simple entropy perhaps, that the alien being will conquer and absorb within itself all that it seeks? It has been written of in *The Ancient Book of Kor*, has it not?"

"Yes it has been written in various prophecies, but while that book and others tell us that no Ares man shall ever defeat the Kin-Ty-Roo, this Jon Kirk is *not* an Ares man."

"Yes, I see that, he is an Earther, an outworlder, but that is just words, minor details at that. These are just old myths at best I think probably not relevant to our modern days," the king countered suspiciously.

"Perhaps, my king, but with Earth and the Sindalki home world now having been destroyed, Ares will certainly be next. And that means our tiny city of Kev here as well. I can not allow that. The Council will not allow that. You can not allow that, my king."

The old men of the Elder Council, each one possessing more galaxy-spanning mind power than almost any other beings in the Known Universe—aside from one mysterious alien entity usually not to be named—nodded their agreement.

"This alien entity, what has been called the Kin-Ty-Roo, what can we do about it?" Shamar asked with deep concern, for he plainly saw the impending danger.

"It must be destroyed, though I know it shall not be a simple matter. I and my mind masters will not be able to do it on our own—though we can help. We must seek help. Jon Kirk may be the only one who may be able to perform the actual deed. So we must do all we can to help him achieve that aim. The Known Universe that we are a part of, is now in a life and death struggle my king, and we must be on the side of life."

"I agree, but what does that truly mean? What are we to do?" the king asked carefully.

"Jon Kirk must first be told about all the knowledge we possess and the full extent of it—and it must all be made available for his use to defeat this Kin-Ty-Roo. We must also tell him the Secret Truths and Lost Histories. All of them. Some even you do not know, my king. Some you can not even imagine. He must know it all, so he can make use of it if need be, and to consider all this information for use in his plan for victory."

"That means letting him—and even myself—know about all your innermost and secret mind powers, the full extent of what the mind masters know," Shamar asked in surprise, for the powers of the mind masters of Kev had been the most jealously guarded secrets on all of Ares—most jealously guarded from all other Greens on the planet and especially from the creatures who had served the Secret Empire of the Hundred Worlds and their Sindalki masters.

"Yes, we must be open and truthful and tell him all of it. We must speak truthfully of the extent of our mind powers to Jon Kirk and make them useful to him in his coming battles. We must also fight for him in the coming battles, and no doubt, some of us will die for him. It must come to pass. We have no choice now but to fight for victory—the only alternative is total extinction of our race and all the races of all the worlds of the Known Universe. We can not accept that. It will all come to pass one way or the other. Jon Kirk is the key."

The king looked at the venerable wise old man who stood so firmly before him, "How do you know that the emperor is even coming here, Aron?"

"It is simple, my king, Jon Kirk and one other are on their way here in a small flier at this very moment. I have already used my mind to contact the emperor and I have given him and his pilot the coordinates to our location. They should be here soon."

"Hah, you are a man of many surprises, Aron! Then this should prove most interesting, should it not?"

"Yes, it should, my king."

"So we wait for Jon Kirk to arrive?"

"Yes, we wait for the emperor to arrive. In the meantime may I have Lord Kneth brought here? He may have some additional light to shed upon the story that I will be telling you, and the emperor. It is a story neither of you have ever heard in full before."

King Shamar nodded, concern etching his features. Allowing Jon Kirk to assume the emperorship was one thing, but now King Shamar's city and people were in danger once again. This time not from Winged-men or Blue Vognar invisible conquerors, nor even from a Secret Empire battle fleet, but from some mysterious entity known as the Kin-Ty-Roo. Shamar wondered what manner of monster such a thing might be if it had been able to corrupt and turn an all powerful Sindalki mind master like Lord Karlath Doom to its dark cause.

CHAPTER 6

The Audience in Kev

The voice within my head was one I recognized well from previous experience. It was that of Aron the Eldest. It was originating from the new city of Kev, that had replaced the ancient lost city of Keva. The city had been known as Keva before it had been destroyed by a Vognar warship in the previous war upon Ares a year ago. Now Lord Aron and the Kevens had rebuilt their city, but this time on the western continent of Vognar. It was a much more secluded land mass. Lord Aron knew we were coming to seek him out and he welcomed us graciously, giving myself and Tor-nul the directions to fly our small craft to his new hidden city. We flew across the raging seas of the Serpent Water ocean and soon received a large land mass and were flying over the western continent within hours.

Tor-nul landed our small flier in a wide open field of tall grass and thin sapling trees. It was an apparently vast empty area. Well, perhaps it was. It certainly appeared to be deserted. Or at least, possibly. I was not all that certain that what I and Tor-nul were seeing with our eyes was truly what was actually there. You could never tell with mind masters. They had the power to cloud men's minds.

"It is most strange, Jon Kirk. I never had the experience of hearing another's voice inside my mind like that," Tor-nul told me a bit nervously as he landed our small flier at the indicated location. We landed the craft and prepared to leave it and look around at the large empty landscape around us.

"I know, my friend, it can be a bit hard to get used to," I replied with a slight grin at the young warrior's surprise at his first encounter with a mind master's incredible talent. He smiled nervously, but nodded bravely. Then we exited our craft and scanned the area. As I expected, I did not see anyone around, and it appeared the field was entirely deserted. It seemed most strange. There was nothing to see, and there was no one there. No one was there at all as far as I could see.

"Yes it is most strange, but he led us directly here. His directions were very specific, but what is this place? I see no city? Nothing at all is here," Tor-nul said suspiciously.

"Yes, and you will see no city, not here, my friend. It is all underground and most secret. We will be approached directly I am sure, just be patient," I told my young warrior companion.

Tor-nul was armed, of course, as was I. We each wore a short Ares sword in a scabbard along with holstered death ray pistols. Tor-nul also carried a powerful death ray rifle, and I, of course, still wore my belted holster holding my U.S. Army Colt .45 Auto. I patted the grips of the weapon lovingly, it and I had been through much together, through the jungles of Vietnam on the Earth, and now here on Ares since I had come to this new world years ago. Our chief scientist, Ras-noor, gave me the means to keep the weapon in top-notch working order and armed with plenty of new bullets. We both also wore small personal shields for protection that we activated now.

"Look, here comes someone now!" Tor-nul alerted me, raising his rifle in a defensive posture.

"Lower your weapon, Tor-nul, we will find none but friends here."

My companion looked at me carefully, "But My Emperor…"

I could see he was concerned for my safety.

"We are safe here, I assure you, now please do as I say."

He nodded and lowered his weapon. His concern for my safety was touching but unnecessary.

I noted the powerfully built but elderly man who was walking towards us. I knew him well. He was alone. Unarmed. There was no one else with him. He needed no others.

"Lord Aron, it is good to see you again, my friend," I said to the wise old Keven who now came boldly towards us with a broad welcoming smile.

"And I you, Jon Kirk, My Emperor. I am happy that you are here. If you and your man will follow me, I will take you to the King. King Shamar is eagerly awaiting your visit and I am sure that you have many questions for us."

"I do. That is why I am here, Lord Aron."

"I know that, Jon Kirk, and that is why we of Kev have brought you here, so we can answer those questions," he told me as he led Tor-ul and I away from our small flier, through the tall grasses and into a nearby wooded grove. As we walked, I wondered at the change in the manners of the mysterious Kevens having suddenly become so friendly and cooperative, but I thought it best for now to leave those questions be. I was sure they would tell me of their plans and feelings in their own good time, but it was apparent that their feelings on some things had certainly changed. And for the better.

"Jon Kirk," Lord Aron spoke up softly, looking deeply into my eyes, "we just heard the terrible news. I am sorry about what happened to your home planet of Earth."

I nodded gravely, "Thank you, my friend, I appreciate your thoughtfulness. Know this, I will take my revenge. I will hunt though all the Known Universe if I must to rid it of this evil scourge that goes by the name of Lord Karlath Doom!"

"Most appropriate, under the circumstances, of course, and I fully agree, but you must also destroy the dark master of Lord Doom, the entity that is called the Kin-Ty-Roo. That is of paramount importance to us all. It is essential to our very survival. Doom is just a minion, a device, an instrument of the far greater and more deadly entity. It is that entity you must concentrate on, for all our sakes, Jon Kirk. That is the true peril."

"I will take care of Lord Doom first," I replied firmly, my mind set.

"Of course," Aron agreed, but I heard a slight dismissive tone in his words. It was then obvious to me that he had a different agenda from my own, but he was acceding to my wishes for the present. So be it. I welcomed any help I could get from him and his people.

Lord Aron next led us into a sudden opening through the grove and tall grasses where we saw what appeared to be a large uplifted door, and inside it many rows of steps that led deeply downward far into the ground below. It was like an open pit down into the very bowels of the planet, or so it seemed. I knew that it could not be anything like that though. It had to be the entrance to their city. It was most mysterious.

"Behold, the entrance to the secret city of Kev," Lord Aron proudly announced to Tor-nul and myself.

Well, what we saw there was not much to look at, but I assume they wanted it that way. If the door was closed and you blinked you might miss the entrance entirely. It would certainly be invisible from the air. Had not Lord Aron given us explicit directions here, and come out to meet us, we would never have found the place at all. Of course the entire city was shielded from all sensor devices and mind scans.

The opening to Kev became a long, deep, wide line of steps reaching ever downward into the ground. They seemed to go very far down. It did not appear to presage very much at all, but once we reached the bottom—of a very long descent of some 500 steps that took us quite a while to walk down—we eventually went towards a guarded heavy door. That door was suddenly opened before us to reveal a large and lush underground facility. Tor-nul and I were amazed by what we saw. It was beautiful! Glorious!

Here was the heart of the secret city of Kev!

I had never seen the likes of anything like this before on Ares or upon Earth. It was immense and expansive, well-lighted; a colorful area, full of blooming plants and green ferns, colorful flowers of all types, delightful fragrances overcame our sense of smell from all manner of lush plant life. It looked to be a wonderful garden full of apparently happy people going about their business. Many of them looked at us and smiled or spoke words of welcome, and all acknowledged Aron the Eldest with deep respect. The place was magnificent!

"My Emperor!" Tor-nul whispered looking around him with awe and amazement writ large upon his face, and then looking back at me, "is this Cali-Nor? Can it be?"

I looked at my young friend and gave him a slight smile, for he had asked me if this place was Cali-Nor, the land that to the green people of Ares roughly conforms to what most Earthers might call Heaven.

"No, my young friend, it is not," I told Tor-nul in a soft voice. "This is not Cali-Nor, though I could see how one might mistake it as such, it is only the secret hidden realm of the Kevens. That is all."

"Well, it is truly amazing!" Tor-nul replied with a look of continued awe as his eyes scanned the area around us. "I had never thought such a wonderful place could ever exist upon Ares."

Lord Aron came over and led us deeper into the heart of his wonderful city.

"Not Cali-Nor, but much like it," I said to Lord Aron.

"That is correct, Jon Kirk, and you, young warrior who serves the emperor, now feast your eyes and behold the secret city of Kev," Aron the Eldest told us with an indulgent but warm glowing smile as his arm made a grand sweeping gesture for us to take in the amazing beauty and wonder of the hidden city of Kev. We saw a large underground valley that stretched on almost forever, underground, caverns, so mysterious, almost magical. "No, it is not Cali-Nor, but it is something close to that for us—it is the last home of the Ancients of Ares. You see, we of Kev are their last remaining direct descendants in every manner. We are the last of the ancient Mind Masters of Ares."

I looked with sudden surprise at Lord Aron. I had heard some rumors and old stories about the vast powers these people possessed but I had never thought they were so closely connected with the mysterious Ancients of Ares, the mental wizards that Tar-gool and Rasnoor had told me about in hushed whispers long ago in secret talks. "You are the last of them then?"

"Yes, we are the last of them, and we have much to tell you. Come, Jon Kirk, and you, young Tor-nul, follow me through the corridors of our beloved city, to the King's audience chamber, where all your questions will be answered. And even some questions you never would have thought to ask."

I looked at Aron the Eldest carefully, taking in the depth of his words and Tor-nul and I silently accompanied him to our audience with the King.

* * * *

King Shamar of Kev met us in a large but Spartan audience chamber. It was good to see the young monarch once again and we embraced each other as old comrades and friends. Shamar and I had been through some tough experiences with the Blues of Vognar in the past and had great respect for each other as fighting men and friends. Zaor had been with us then too. We were old and good allies from that past war. It was good to see him now and looking so well. He was not alone. The King of Kev was surrounded by all of the Council of Elders of the Keven people, those venerables who were known as the mind masters.

I was also surprised to notice Lord Kneth sitting silently with a person I deemed to be a nurse or health attendant. He did not acknowledge our presence, and in fact the powerful Sindalki lord seemed to be as ill and in dire consequences as he had been since he had discovered the truth about Lord Doom's treachery against his fleet, and the murder of his entire race. His home world had been destroyed. That destruction had caused a massive sickness within him that had taken hold of Lord Kneth, and now I too felt that same sickness within me. It was a deep emptiness, an utter void within my heart, from the destruction of the Earth. Doom had a lot to answer for but I could conceive of no punishment dreadful enough to inflict upon him for his great crimes.

"Come this way, Jon Kirk, and I will introduce you to our people," Lord Aron stated as he guided me and Tor-nul forward among a group of distinguished older Kevens—the Mind Masters who held such great mental powers and bowed before us.

"King Shamar, it is good to see you again, my friend," I told the young Keven monarch. He was a youthful warrior chosen by the Elders for his brave battle skills, but one whose mind power potential I had been told was vast—but as yet not fully developed. He would undergo more intensive mind training in the future. Meanwhile, Aron the Eldest, the sage and leader of the Council of Elders, the most powerful man possessing mind powers on the planet Ares, introduced Tor-nul and myself to all who were in attendance at the meeting. There was much joy shown by them in meeting us and realizing we were now all allies in the great war to come.

My eyes could not help but stray to the sad Sindalki survivor, Lord Kneth, the last one of his people left alive—other than the hated monster Lord Doom. I felt a great sadness for this man now, knowing exactly what he was going through. For anyone to have his entire home world destroyed was a terrible event that marked your mind with heavy damage and crippled your heart forever. I wondered if there could ever be recovery for him—or myself—from such horror.

"How is his health?" I asked Lord Aron, indicating the seemingly lifeless Sindalki lord.

"Physically he has recovered somewhat, but emotionally not so much at all. I fear he is going downward into a dark deep spiral that he shall not come out of. He carries a heavy burden—guilt and a black sadness the depths to which we can not reach, even with our vast mind powers—and even with his own powers. He has given up, I am afraid, and he may soon expire if something is not done to revive his inner spirit."

I nodded, I could well understand how he felt now. I also realized that I was perhaps the only person there who could fully comprehend what Lord Kneth was going through. I decided to openly contact this last Sindalki nobleman. I would speak with him and see what I could do to ease his suffering.

Lord Kneth had been the Secret Empire fleet representative of the 'No Faction', and Lord Doom had been the leader of the Sindalki Secret Empire fleet. Doom had been the leader of the victorious 'Yes Faction' of the Sindalki and as such held full command. I had since learned that the Sindalki lords for all their vast and destructive mind powers employed a rather simple but effective means of control and consensus to rule their empire without ever having to resort to civil war or rebellion—but they had not fully contemplated the results of treason. The lords simply voted and the victors appointed a representative to lead them, however the losing side in any argument was also included as part of any action by furnishing their own representative. So all Sindalki were involved and represented in every action they undertook, and so all were united in that manner. It seemed an effective way of ruling without resorting to rebellion. A least, for a time. Then Lord Karlath Doom came along.

I learned the 'Yes Faction' had won the vote for war with Ares long ago and had taken the lead in all things for a long time, however the 'No Faction'—that always loses the vote—was still always represented. Hence the Sindalki lords are always of one mind and worked together in any action they undertook. They maintained a united front in all things.

The plan to gather the fleet to do battle with the Enemy Empire of the Kin-Ty-Roo, and to punish Ares and myself for freeing my adopted world of the dread Winged-men of Zar—just one world in the sweeping Secret Empire—had been Lord Doom's plan. But it had been a ruse. He had desired all along to gather the fleet in orbit around Ares upon the pretext of punishing Ares, but his real plan had been to betray his own battle fleet so that they could be defeated by the warships of the enemy entity known as the Kin-Ty-Roo. I had complicated that plan and eventually caused it to fail. No doubt that had been the impetus for much of his enmity against me.

With these thoughts in mind I walked over to Lord Kneth and quietly sat down beside him. I remained silent for a long moment formulating my thoughts. This Sindalki lord, like all of his kind, could be uncooperative, difficult, and supremely arrogant. However, I did not come here to parse my words or my thoughts, and I felt Lord Kneth's mind now delicately and softly within my own. I heard his voice within my mind as soft and clear, curious, as though he were speaking the words from his own lips.

"It is you?" he whispered softly.

"Yes," I told him.

"Well, you are correct, Jon Kirk, you are the only being who can truly comprehend my overwhelming pain and sadness. It is a most debilitating effect," Lord Kneth's mind spoke into my own. No words were spoken verbally.

I nodded, I did not vocalize my answer, but instead tried this most intimate and personal way of communicating that I had learned a year ago from the wily Tar-gool and more recently from Aron the Eldest. I answered Lord Kneth in mind-speak, all I had to do was project my thoughts as silent words within my mind into his own. "I appreciate your pain and suffering, for I feel it as well."

"I know that you do, I can see it within you."

"I am sorry for the loss of your world, and your noble people," I told him sincerely.

"And I am sorry for what was done to the Earth. It should never have happened. You see, we Sindalki are not all as arrogant and power-mad as Lord Doom and his faction would make us. Sadly they are a majority among us, a group of greedy power seekers, but they do not represent all of us."

"I see that now, Lord Kneth. I see it there inside you, in your heart and in your mind. I can see the kind of man you are and I see the pain and guilt you wear as such a heavy burden," I told him respectfully.

"And I see you too, Jon Kirk, as Lord Aron and the Kevens see you, the true you, so full of doubt. I tell you now, there is nothing to fear, for you are a great warrior, and very brave, but you are a man sometimes confused as how to act. I see great strength and goodness in you. You are truly the man to be our emperor. Lord Aron chose wisely, so you should cast aside all doubt about your assumption of power and firmly embrace your proper role as our emperor. Do not doubt yourself any longer."

I nodded, masking my doubts as his words rang true to me. I told him, "It is hard for me to accept this burden, my friend. But if I do so, then will you do the same, Lord Kneth?"

"Me? What can I do? I am but one shattered Sindalki lord, alone and worldless now, who is hoping to soon take the final voyage to see my ancestors."

"Not for a long time, I pray. I ask you now to join me by taking up the mantle of the fight against Lord Doom and the entity that made him perform his evil deed against the world of Sindalki. Take your fight to him."

"I cannot!"

"Do it for justice!"

"I have not the strength nor desire."

"Then do it because it is what is right."

"I do not care any longer about concepts such as right and wrong. I am apathetic and await my end."

"No, your end will not come for a long time," I told him sharply.

He shook his head. There was no reply either verbal or through mind speak.

I looked at the Sindalki lord, as my mind dug down deep into the heart of his mind, the soul of his mind, and I saw a dead black spot there that I knew I could reach and cause to come to life. I knew that I could cause it to come to life in a most unusual way. It could be dangerous to set the Sindalki on this course, but I would take the chance now.

"Then do it for something much more concrete—for something truly real—do it for bloody revenge!" I mind-spoke to him fiercely, allowing my full fury to vent.

Lord Kneth looked over at me seriously, actually startled, surprised by my harsh words and the anger in my request. He now spoke openly to me, verbally, "Revenge? You are sure about this? You believe this to be the proper way?"

"Proper? Revenge? I do not know, and I do not care. However, it is perhaps the only way for you now, my friend. I will destroy Lord Doom, and while it will surely be for many altruistic reasons—reasons we all share as he certainly deserves punishment and destruction—it will be for one stark personal reason. A reason often more powerful than all others—sheer revenge. Join me in that revenge, Lord Kneth—and I will join you in your own. Together we will make Doom pay for his evil deeds against our worlds and our people! Let us punish him as he deserves! Let us avenge those he has so callously murdered!"

Lord Kneth looked me squarely in the face, eye to eye. The fire was now aglow in his eyes, his jaw set firm and his lips held tight. There was great power within him and controlled focused anger now. I could feel the rage and surge of hatred igniting deep within him. That small black spot in him was growing in size, becoming red as if ignited and now on fire.

He was getting mad. Angry. Furious.

Good!

He was quiet for a long moment, apparently thinking it all through in his own Sindalki manner. He looked at me sadly, then the fire of anger overtook his features.

"There is no more Sindalki world, no more Secret Empire of the Hundred Worlds, there is only you, Jon Kirk, so now I serve you, My Emperor," he spoke firmly looking at me with deep and serious meaning.

I was surprised by his steadfast words of loyalty and conviction. I had only asked for his help, not his absolute fealty for my being his lord and emperor, but he did not waver in his desire to serve me now. He stood up tall and straight, then lowered himself to one knee and said solemnly, "I have seen the inside world of your mind, Jon Kirk, and it is good. I shall follow you and do all I can to contribute to your success in this quest for revenge, as emperor of all the worlds that we call the Known Universe. So be it. We shall seek our revenge, together!"

I hardly knew what to say to that. Lord Aron, King Shamar, Tornul and the others came over to us much surprised at hearing these words but full of joy by Lord Kneth's action and to see his apparent revival back to the world of the living. It was good to see him recovered and now fully with us in the coming battle. His alliance was most important and welcome.

"You have brought him back to us, Jon Kirk," Lord Aron told me gratefully, "Only you could have done it."

"I just spoke to him, man to man, and he…"

"He is necessary to the plan," Lord Aron told me simply.

"I will now help you in any way that I am able, Jon Kirk, My Emperor," Lord Kneth spoke up firmly, decisively, "and you must now listen carefully for there is much you must be told about. Is that not true, Lord Aron?"

Aron the Eldest just nodded his agreement silently, and I wondered what was going on now in his own mind. His inner thoughts were now closed off to me.

"Good, then I believe that Lord Aron, you should tell Jon Kirk the Ares part of the story and I shall tell the Sindalki part of the story, and then our emperor will know all of the story of the history of the worlds that make up the Known Universe and beyond, that he rules now."

I looked from Lord Aron to Lord Kneth and back to Aron quite surprised by this. What was it all about? Something most strange for sure. I knew that I would soon find out and I believed that when I realized what it was all about it would prove to be a mind-blasting realization. A game changer. And it surely proved to be that, which I am not exaggerating in any way.

It began like this…

CHAPTER 7

Aron the Eldest Speaks

"My Emperor," King Shamar spoke up once we were all comfortably seated in his massive audience chamber and drinks had been brought over, "there is much you need to know. Of course there is the traditional history, but there is also much secret history—and then, additionally, there is that which is called by some, The Most Secret History."

That last phrase got my attention.

"The Most Secret History?" I asked Shamar with unabated suspicion. The king did not reply to my question, so my eyes immediately focused upon Lord Aron firmly and I saw him nod at me ominously with a wry grin. I wondered just what they were up to.

Aron the Eldest told me guardedly, "Yes, and the Most Secret History is the most difficult knowledge of all to speak of, My Emperor." I could see he was held by some reluctance on this matter for a man such as Lord Aron surely did not want to speak of these things, but he knew that he must, so he was obviously conflicted, but then resolved to do so. In fact, he needed to speak of it. So be it.

I only nodded for the moment, wondering just what I was in for.

"So then, you begin it, Lord Aron, and spare me and the Sindalki people no harsh truth in your telling of it all and complete," Lord Kneth said boldly.

"So be it," Lord Aron replied to the Sindalki lord, taking a moment to collect his thoughts. He looked at me rather sadly I thought. I wondered why. What the hell was coming?

"There is much to tell, Jon Kirk. All the secrets shall come out now, some strange, some too dire to behold, but all of it true. So let me begin the telling now. Are you ready?"

"Yes," I whispered a bit hoarsely wondering just what was I was in for.

"Know this, as I speak these words verbally, I also speak them within your mind, and into the minds of all those who are here. You will be shown many mental images, truly terrible images inside your mind to go along with my words. My words will describe what has happened in the past. My images are transferred from my mind into yours, originally taken from the minds of our ancient ancestors from long ago in the far away past. These words and images will show you exactly what they saw happen in those long ago days. You will see them and feel them just as the Ancients of Ares did when it all happened. It will be difficult. Do you understand?"

"Yes, I think so," I answered, not really quite sure what to expect.

I looked over at Tor-nul. He just nodded, but I could see he was nervous about what I might be shown. As it turned out he was lucky, for he would not privileged receive any of the images or information that would be given now, but I could see he was intensely curious, though he did not say one word.

"I tell you, Jon Kirk, do not fear these images. Know that as extreme and real as they may appear, they are but images, shades from the past, and they are not from the here and now. They can not harm you," Lord Aron explained carefully.

I nodded, curious, careful.

However, next he did warn me, "but the images you will see are very powerful. Extremely disturbing. You will feel them just as our ancestors did. You will fell the severe measure of the pain and anger they instill. They can infect the mind with sadness and grim despair, they can damage a mind not prepared to see and feel such things and guard against them—for it will seem as real to you as if you were there when it happened to our people so long ago. It will seem as if it happened to *you*. You will feel it all. So be forewarned."

I nodded. "I understand. Let us begin."

"Yes, then begin it," King Shamar ordered.

Lord Aron nodded.

Suddenly my mind was inundated and overwhelmed by such vast sensory input I was totally shocked, shaken, appalled by the very force and fury of the images. The bright colors, the intense sounds, the feelings of great anger and hatred were incredible. The sheer amount of information, voices, words, and stark visual imagery was overwhelming and I cried out in pain. I had not expected this at all.

It was mind numbing and mind expanding at the same time. Even hallucinogenic drugs were not as real or hard-hitting as what I saw now within my mind, infecting my very thoughts. Nothing like this seemed conceivable unless it had come out of the dark pit of sheer madness and I began to wonder, if in fact, I had gone mad.

The fearful thought resounded within my mind and threatened to unnerve me.

Had I gone mad?

"No, Jon Kirk, you are not mad," a calm voice told me reassuringly.

Then I saw standing there beside me, within the portal of my mind, the images of Aron the Eldest and Lord Kneth. It was Lord Aron who spoke to me in a soft comforting voice, "We are here to guide you on this journey. Fear not, we will protect you and show you all that you need to see and know."

I nodded, shaking a bit in subdued terror, and I am sure my face had turned a rather sad shade of pale. I was now sweating profusely. I had been pushed to the edge by the horrors I had seen and felt as if real, but now I was gently led back to a safer place. I relaxed and took in all the information—the amazing and violent images one by one more slowly—it was so very much to see!—so very terrible and violent—but I learned.

"You are our emperor, you need to see it all, you need to know it all, to feel it all, Jon Kirk," Lord Kneth whispered into my subconscious mind. "You need to feel it all as if it truly happened to you. That is the only way for you to fully comprehend what happened and what you—and all of us—are up against."

And then I was able to see and feel it all and I learned the truth. All the truth—or all the various truths. All the history, the secret history, and even that which was secluded as the Most Secret History.

I will not bore you with the many facts and plethora of stark terrifying images, the pain and extreme violence that went along with the long ago story of Ares. The glorious civilization that had once thrived upon the planet Ares. It had been a bright spot in the long run of the surge of humanity in the upward climb for civilization. For a time that bright spot shone in the vast area of Known Space.

Then had come the genocidal extermination of the Ancients of Ares!

These Ancients of Ares were both green and blue hued people, a race whose civilization had attained a high level of power and success. These Ancients harnessed what they called the Three Forms of Power. These were known by them as three separate modes for action.

Physical Action, was the first of these and was self explanatory. The people of Ares were warriors after all and proficient with swords and spears and all manner of physical things. They built things, made war, fought battles.

Next was Scientific Action, which included the super science that allowed them to make powerful weapons and design great machines to improve their lives. It allowed them to travel the stars.

The last and most important of the Three Forms of Power was Mental. Mind Action. The Mind Masters of Ares, through their great thought and mental powers, could communicate far and wide, and through the melding of their minds they could accomplish amazing things. Their melding of minds could increase that power a hundred-fold—even a thousand fold. They were capable of incomprehensible things.

This was all tens of thousands of years ago, when the Ares civilization flourished and grew, even expanding beyond the borders of their home world. Using their mind powers the Ancients of Ares were even able to communicate with beings on other worlds and learn about them. Using their super-science they were able to build and send out mighty ships into the empty and dark void between the planets and eventually seed faraway planets with colonies of their own people. These colonies grew and thrived.

The Ares civilization of long ago expanded and became a beacon for civilization throughout what we now call the Known Universe. I saw visions of gleaming cities that shone with brightness and glory all over Ares, and cities and settlements upon other worlds that were most lovely but very strange to me. These were images of far away worlds that shone with the glory of the ancient civilization of Ares. The people of Ares were always bold, supremely confident, generous and inquisitive about others and everything in their world, as well as the universe around them. They used their super-science—which had advanced far beyond anything ever known on my own world of Earth—along with their vast mind powers unknown on Earth—

to perform miraculous actions. Never believing themselves to be gods—for they despised such arrogance a terrible blasphemy—they accepted that all their good fortune derived from a beneficent creator who looked upon all the people of Ares with great love and affection. They felt their duty as a civilization was to share their gifts with other intelligent races on the many planets they came across. Including a young race of mind masters, who called themselves the Sindalki.

"It was truly a golden age for Ares, Jon Kirk," Aron the Eldest spoke into my mind, but suddenly a great sadness and remorse was overcoming his words, "but like all golden ages—as in all things—there is always a beginning—and so there must also be an end. Lord Kneth, perhaps you should begin now?"

CHAPTER 8

Lord Kneth Speaks

Suddenly there was a great silence, it was as if an empty void had manifested itself within my mind. I seemed to float for a moment, quiet, calm, and then everything all rushed in upon me. I was struck first by the hard feeling of it all; the shock, the bloody violence, intense greed—such extensive greed! Then vile hatred, fear, loathing, and always more violence and brutal death. Unimaginable death caused by ever more vicious terrible bloody killing.

It was the results of the Sindalki!

Lord Kneth's voice now rang though my mind like a loud bell. It was strong and commanding, but sad and I detected not only sorrow in it, but a sense of great regret and a mighty, almost limitless, guilt. He was showing and telling me the story of his own people now, but he did not agree with most of it at all. That spoke well of him in my eyes.

"My Emperor, the Sindalki were also an advanced race, living upon the planet Sindalki, and we had achieved our own high state of civilization—though we did not have in our hands or minds all the powerful secrets of the Ancients of Ares. We were not an overtly physical race of beings, we did not fight battles with swords and spears or train as warriors in the martial arts of the Physical Realm as those on Ares did. Their's was a planet of battle and war, even though one of high civilization. The two are not incompatible—in fact, they may indeed each be essential for the success of any great civilization. We Sindalki were more abstract thinkers, talkers, traders, and to be honest…simply sheer opportunists. We were cunning. We had our own super-science and we had some mind powers, though nothing as extensive as those then possessed by the Ancients of Ares. At least, not at first."

Lord Kneth stopped for a moment, I could feel great regret surrounding his thoughts. Then he sighed and continued. "It was those from Ares who contacted us first. They had found us you see, and they seemed to feel that we had some potential to aid them in their bid for the expansion of civilization throughout the Known Universe. They were peaceful and logical. We could see right away that they had much to teach us. We saw the advantages. Some partnership soon developed. We encouraged the contact, the free exchange of information, especially knowledge of their fantastical very advanced mind powers.

"The Ancients of Ares were truly mind masters and we quickly realized that if we were ever to best them we must become powerful mind masters as well. However, we also realized the only way we could defeat them, conqueror them—for that is what our plan had been all along—we needed to be patient and learn all we could from them. We did. We pretended friendship. We fawned loyalty. Then once ready, our 'Yes Faction' would give the command for us to act and take Ares down with a three pronged attack."

Lord Kneth sighed mightily, "Of course our attack encompassed the Three Realms of Power. That included overt physical action, as well as using our own super-science; and it was bolstered by our own vast mind powers—for soon we had our own mind masters who had learned only too well from the people of Ares. In fact, it came to pass that our super-science powers became equal to their own. So we knew those powers, and those weapons, could cancel each other out in any battle. This was a problem for some of us."

"In time, we learned the secrets of the people of Ares and their mind powers. The free and good people of Ares were always such generous teachers—and we eventually matched them there as well. So there was another stalemate. We eventually had them stymied in the area of mind power as well."

The Sindalki lord continued. "However, it was on the Physical Plane of Power where we lacked effective resources that could guarantee us victory, for we were not warriors and the Ancients of Ares were experts in the use of all manner of physical actions and weapons. They were true warriors. Bold fighters. They were supremely confident in their martial abilities, without being arrogant. Those of Ares were noble warriors, but also teachers and friends—and my people betrayed them. It was a great shame to me. It happened this way. We realized that their military prowess could make an essential difference in our plan of invasion and conquest and could thwart our victory. And then we hit upon the perfect plan."

I looked over at Lord Kneth, tears were now flowing from his eyes, red bloody tears. I shook, I had heard enough, seen enough. The images I now saw and felt were terrible, horrible scenes of vile betrayal, violence, murder on a scale unimaginable, but there was more. Worse.

Lord Kneth's mind spoke softly into mine now, sad with sorrow, "Once the Sindalki matched the Ancients of Ares in super-science and mind powers—we realized that in essence these powers could cancel each other out in the fury of action and battle. Something else was needed. Something more. That left us the Physical Plane of Power. That meant personal battle on the ground, down and dirty, actual physical combat against the people of Ares with swords and spears, fierce fighting in hand to hand killing. It meant the death of them all. Fighting. Murder. Genocide! It was the final and necessary ingredient we knew that would lead to our complete victory. However, we despaired of ever winning such a physical battle on our own—our warriors were no match for those of Ares—and then we came upon the Winged-men of Zar.

Lord Kneth shook his head and looked at me closely, inside my mind and heart, touching my soul and the pulse of my life. He lowered his gaze, then continued. "We immediately realized the monstrous and savage creatures from Zar were the perfect agents for the physical part of our attack upon the warriors of Ares, so we brought the Winged-men there and set them loose upon the planet. And so we betrayed our loyal benefactors and friends. While the powers of super-science and our mind masters tended to cancel each other out in the final battle for control—once we brought the Winged-men of Zar to Ares and set them lose, they created utter havoc. They murdered our old friends on a horrendous scale."

Lord Kneth shook his head despondently, "We betrayed them! The Ares fighters were brave but overwhelmed, unable to stand up against the onslaught of the vicious Winged-men, deadly monsters whom we directed. In time the Winged-men would conquer all of Ares and become our allies. We won the war and then set to work destroying the Ancients of Ares. The war ended, but the Winged-men of Zar still ran rampant with utter destruction and bloody murder, and the Ancients of Ares were soon defeated. No quarter was given. Most of their people were hunted down and killed. Simply exterminated. You see, we could not allow any of them to live—to recover and seek their revenge upon us. Over time the super-science of Ares was lost; the mind powers of the people of Ares were long forgotten; and the Winged-men of Zar ruled the planet and the descendents of those who remained alive in an orgy of bloodlust and violence under our direction. This ensured that Ares would never return to its former ancient glory and that the world of Sindalki, and the Sindalki lords, reigned supreme throughout all the worlds that made up the Known Universe."

The images of death and destruction stopped, thankfully, for they had shattered my mind with the Sindalki lord's narration. Now there was silence for a brief moment.

"I can not believe all this," I stated in anger, my natural skepticism showing.

"There is more," Lord Aron told me.

"These are events and actions I am least proud of," I heard Lord Kneth's voice continue in a low tone. "Some of us tried to stop the betrayal of course, as well as the war against our friends—for some of us did see the Ancients of Ares as friends—but the 'No Faction' was just too weak and the 'Yes Faction' was far too powerful and greedy for conquest. Greed dominated, power was as a drug for too many of our powerful lords. There could be no other result."

There was silence for a moment longer, while within my head the images ceased. I took a deep breadth, I had seen such utter chaos and brutality, such terrible warfare as I had never thought possible. Bloody murder, horrendous destruction, utter chaos.

Lord Kneth resumed. "Thus began what would become the Secret Empire of the Hundred Worlds, ruled behind the scenes by the Sindalki lords. We spread our ships and fleet to conqueror planet after planet, and many races from many other worlds. The Winged-men of Zar became a part of our empire, and were used as fighters in our army and fleet. The Gorms and Blue Kortas as well. We conquered all who stood before us and incorporated them into our military—or we destroyed them."

Now another image came sharply into my mind. It was an image I recognized immediately. It was the Earth! But it was not the Earth I knew from my present day, it was the Earth of tens of thousands of years ago when there had been but one massive continent upon the planet. Earth looked lovely, a single green and brown land mass surrounded by bright blue oceans, and then my mind was shown images far beyond my home world; and I recognized them as the Moon, and then Mars—which was strangely brightly lit and *green*—and then there was *another* world. Where had it come from? It was a world I had never seen before. A world I had never even dreamed existed before. It was another lovely blue planet, perhaps a water world, and it was set in orbit between Mars and Jupiter   it was a planet located where we on Earth now call the Asteroid Belt.

I looked at Lord Kneth sharply, he just nodded and continued his explanation, "These were all Ancient Ares colonies in your Sol System. Of course, our military plans made it plain that they all had to be eliminated. The main Ares colony, a thriving world of many millions of inhabitants was the fifth planet from the sun, a world called Vulcan. It was totally obliterated. The remnants of it now exist as lifeless rock forming an asteroid belt. The planet you call Mars had a lesser colony, and it was destroyed, its atmosphere torn away and thrust out into the void of space. The planet left a dead and dry red rock. And the third Ares colony, a far smaller one built upon the single continent of Atlantis upon your Earth, Jon Kirk, was destroyed and sunk, the large land mass broken apart in cataclysmic destruction. Thus the Secret Empire and the Sindalki lords eliminated the Ancients of Ares, along with all their space colonies forever."

"Ahem!" I heard the sound come from Lord Aron.

"Yes, you are correct," Lord Kneth added a bit shyly, "it is true, we never suspected that the people of Keva were the last descendants of the Ancients of Ares—we did not know that they were the last of the Mind Masters. Our Winged-men allies never found their secret city. We would have destroyed them too had we known of their existence, or been able to find them."

"I am sure you would have," Lord Aron stated looking at Lord Kneth sharply.

"So there you have it, Jon Kirk," King Shamar told me with a deep sigh. "What do you think of it all?"

I hardly knew what to think. I looked around at the faces of each of the men in that room. I could barely believe what I had just been told—what I had just seen in so many vivid mental images that were as clear to me as if I had been right there when it had all happened ages ago. I was astounded by it all, and so very sad. I felt the pain and it lived within me now in searing memories, as if the memories were my own. It was…difficult to deal with. Now I knew much of the secret past history of Earth, and of the Sol System—and the fact that humanity had all once come from the world of Ares.

I looked at the men in that room thoughtfully, "What do I think? What do I think about it all! I have no idea what to say, or how to deal with it!"

I was shouting, I was angry, enraged, I looked with the fire of hatred burning in my eyes at Lord Kneth, the Sindalki—and then the fire died for I knew that none of this had been under his order, nor the desire of his faction, to cause this massive betrayal and destruction.

"I am sorry for your world, Jon Kirk," Lord Kneth told me verbally, and I knew that any such sincere apology from a Sindalki lord was a rare thing indeed.

"I—I understand, and I—I see now the connections between Earth and Ares goes far deeper than just one man being transported here a few years ago who has now become a leader on this world."

"An emperor," King Shamar reminded me.

I nodded, trying to un-jumble the information still swirling within my mind, thoughts and stark images that now clouded my thinking. What I had learned and seen was amazing and yet inconceivable.

"Yes," Lord Aron said softly, "it does go much deeper."

I spoke up firmly, "So it is not all about me, it is about Ares, and all the other planets and peoples of the old empire—and the new—of this new empire we are all a part of. I want our people to be free, I want them all to be safe. I want to protect these worlds and their people."

"Then Jon Kirk, you must defeat Lord Doom, and then you must kill the alien entity that is his master," Lord Kneth told me simply.

I looked at them all dubiously. That was a very tall order.

"We will help you," Aron the Eldest added sympathetically, as if reading my thoughts.

I nodded, still overcome by the shock of what I had just seen and learned.

"Yes, and I will help you, as well," Lord Kneth stated forcefully now. "We Sindalki have learned a thing or two since our betrayal of the Ancients of Ares. That knowledge will all be placed at your disposal to defeat Lord Doom and this alien infestation known as the Kin-Ty-Roo."

CHAPTER 9

Forewarned is Forearmed

The thing was, I had received far too much information to digest most of it without some time having to pass. I needed time to think about what I had been told and shown so I could properly digest what I had learned. My mind was still reeling from that knowledge. The one thing I understood clearly, was the enemy that I must destroy. The war that was coming. The sheer enormity of the mission for me now against our enemies seemed impossible. My thoughts concentrated upon this mission, but they also kept harking back to the destruction of the Earth, the death of my friends and all the people I knew who were now lost and gone to me forever. A vast sadness overtook me then, but I had to shake it off in order to keep my mind focused on what was important now—protecting Ares. Saving my people.

I fought a battle within myself to firm up my will and to keep my thoughts focused upon Ares and the new life I had here now. Earth was gone, Ares must be my main concern now. My thoughts centered firmly upon my beloved wife Sirah, our son Alun, true friends and comrades like Zaor, Sahn-jor and Ras-noor. I even thought of my newest friend and ally—Quarto-Zar, Admiral of the fleet—and of all the things he was a Winged-man from Zar! Who would have ever thought such a friendship possible? Not I! The universe was certainly proving to be a most amazing place.

And in the middle of it all was the fight between myself and Lord Karlath Doom, and behind him, the unknown entity called the Kin-Ty-Roo. I had no idea what I was up against, and I knew I had little powers of my own to do much to further my cause for victory. It was true I was an emperor, and in taking on that role I had united our people, but I had very little actual power of my own in this realm of action. I knew I would need to formulate our plan of battle, and soon

I would set the wheels in motion and get ready for war on a scale no world had ever seen before.

My saving grace was the knowledge that Lord Kneth was fully recovered and avidly working with us now. His quest for revenge on Lord Doom had given him new strength and great resolve, a bold purpose for life and action. I did not care at all that it was revenge that primarily motivated him—for it was revenge that also fiercely motivated me as well. Revenge could be good. It could prove most useful. Revenge against Doom for all that he had done against myself and Sirah, and the danger he placed my wife and son—and my adopted world in—but also for what he had done to the Earth. I could never forget that.

How could I ever forget the Earth! The thought of what I had seen done to the planet of my birth would haunt me for the rest of my life. I had not realized the danger my home world had been in, until it had been too late. Now, was it too late for Ares as well? I feared the answer to that question. Now it was time to protect Ares, and then kill Doom before he made his move—before he destroyed us all.

Those were the dark thoughts worming their way through the maze of my mind at the time. Of course, victory in this war was much easier said than done, because it was not so many days before that I had actually killed Lord Doom in a personal battle using my own short sword. That had been when only physical power had been in play, and that fact had been crucial in my fight—especially since at the time super-science and mind powers had been made equal, and stalemated by Lord Aron, so they had been ineffective in any use against me. It was then that the Physical Plane became crucial and crucial for my fight. It seemed as if it had been so long ago now, for had I not just learned how the Sindalki had used the Winged-men of Zar to destroy the Ancients of Ares using mere physical force? Warfare upon the physical realm can prove most effective when other powers have been neutralized, have not been brought into play, or have been made equal and thus ineffectual.

Now the Sindalki were all gone but for two lone survivors. What a shame. What a loss. Though they would not be missed by many. The Sindalki and their hated Secret Empire of the Hundred Worlds were better dead and gone now as far as I was concerned—except that they left something even worse and more deadly and powerful rampantly devouring its way through the Known Universe—the Kin-Ty-Roo. The entity had already devastated a wide area of Known Space that was now called the Empty Quarter. It had invaded the vast sea of space we called the Known Universe and was pressing towards into our empire, towards our worlds—and to Ares. It was here, now, on the attack. Whatever the hell it was, it was on the way towards us. No one seemed to know much about this mysterious alien entity or the vast empire it seemed to control. I decided that it was about time that I found out everything I could about it.

I ordered Lord Kneth to work closely with Lord Aron and the Council of Keven mind masters—they worked in a hidden vault in their secret underground city. I ordered them to get me answers on just what this Kin-Ty-Roo might be. This Thing That Was Not To Be Named, as it was sometimes called by the inhabitants upon other worlds in Known Space. The empire this entity controlled was vast. The fleet of ships under its control was enormous, perhaps more than one thousand warships of all types, from all kinds of worlds. Most of these warships seemed to be from outside our galaxy and I wondered just where they had come from originally. There was an enormous area throughout space that this entity controlled, and I wanted to know all about it now.

"I want you to find out everything about this entity, the bound of the area it controls, and how it is able to control it," I ordered the Council of Mind Masters.

"We can accomplish some of what you want, My Emperor," Lord Aron told me thoughtfully, but seemingly hedging his bets. He and his people did not have ultimate power and I had to remind myself of that fact. "We can mind meld with Lord Kneth and that can give us the power to send our searchings out far and wide. We will map the entity worlds, determine their power, seek out the creature and gently, and most carefully, probe as closely as we dare around it for information."

"Can you kill it?" I asked hopefully, getting to the topic that most interested me. It was the nub of the matter for me.

Lord Aron allowed a slight smile, "My Emperor, we can not even touch it, we dare not get within one light year of it. To do so would risk immediate loss of our control over our own selves—forfeiting our own minds irrevocably to it is will."

"We can not allow that," I stated firmly.

"Agreed," Lord Aron replied sharply.

"Do you think that it can exert control over our people here?" I asked the Keven, alert at the prospect of some kind of alien mind powers used against us—or used to control us.

"It may be possible, though there is no evidence of that as yet. Such control could mean instant death certainly, should the entity desire that, but more likely complete absorption of all beings within the gravity well deep inside the entity. However, I assume the entity may be able to simply take over a mind, to control it, or influence it, and thus use it for its own purposes—if we get too close to it. If so, those unlucky enough to become absorbed could end up working for the entity. Through this control, our enemy may also gain all our knowledge and plans, all our information, and it will surely use all this knowledge to carry out its devious desires. There is great danger in getting too close to this thing, so I want to forewarn you. It is good that we have Lord Kneth with us in this venture. He is fully com-mitted and his talent is of a devious kind that is much needed. His Sindalki powers offer us added strength and a cunning direction we do not possess. He can also be of great value in tracking down Lord Doom, which I know you want to have done as soon as possible."

"Yes, Lord Doom. He is my prime target right now. I want to take care of him first. Find him, Lord Aron! Find out what he has been up to. He has destroyed the Earth, but he has also threatened Ares—though he has not attacked us here yet. I am surprised that he has not yet sent his fleet to destroy Ares. I wonder why. I need to know why. I am sure Ares is his next target."

"I am sure you are correct, Jon Kirk," Lord Aron told me.

"Then why has he not attacked us here yet?"

"I do not know," the Keven replied, his passive face almost blank.

Lord Kneth who was looking on, then spoke up, "There may be another way. Lord Doom is devious. He knows your fleet is here, along with the powerful planetary defenses you have built atop the mountains of Ares. This world is well secure now. He knows an at-tack by his fleet, even as vast and powerful as it may be, will precipi-tate an incredible battle with many losses. Perhaps he does not want to incur that amount of loss—even to attain the victory he seeks?"

"Hah, well that does not seem like the Lord Doom I know, a man who has no care at all for those who serve him," I stated with harsh truth.

"No it is not. He may be seeking to save the fleet for some other purpose, or…" Lord Kneth added, then quietly ended his words.

"Or what?" I asked him curiously. I wondered what the Sindalki lord was getting at. Perhaps only one Sindalki best knew the inner workings of another Sindalki?

"Well, he may have some other plan," Lord Kneth told me enigmatically.

I nodded, I knew that had to be true, but right now I wanted—I needed—answers. Real and concrete answers. What other plan? I needed to know what Doom was up to, then suddenly a cold chill overtook me. "Do you think that even now he has outflanked us and the ships of his fleet are attacking the home planets of our allies—attacking their helpless home worlds?"

"We have not heard of any such attacks taking place, Jon Kirk," Lord Aron stated carefully, but I could see that the thought disturbed him greatly.

"Yes, that is true, but it may be possible, as anything is possible with such a monster—but I think it not very probable at this time, My Emperor," Lord Kneth told me confidently, allowing some of his Sindalki arrogance to show in his tone. "Lord Doom would like to retake our ally worlds and place them under his control once more, if it is possible. I believe he does not seek to destroy them outright, just yet. He is devious enough to know they could prove most useful to him. They, and the vast slave populations he would make of their inhabitants, could prove most valuable if brought back under his control—but only once he has destroyed you, Jon Kirk—and, of course, the planet Ares. No, he is seeking some way to attack Ares, but to do it in a manner to eliminate any danger to his fleet from your own ships or our planetary defenses."

I thought about this and grew more concerned, realizing the bastard was up to something even more devious and unexpected than I thought possible. What could it be? I was sure it would be another no-good shenanigan that might be the end of us all—and it was killing me that I had no idea what it might be!

CHAPTER 10 LORD DOOM ATTACKS

It was a stroke of brilliance. I had to admit it, even as it froze the blood in my veins and caused me to feel a cold shiver run down my back. The very thought had never occurred to me, nor evidently anyone else on my close circle of advisors and the staff of ministers who made up my inner circle who helped me rule our new empire.

Sahn-jor first brought it to my attention, when he called for our greatest scientist, Ras-noor, to visit me in my royal audience chamber in the palace in Tarcos, the capitol city of our empire. All my ministers and advisors, along with many of the leaders of all the associated worlds were present in yet another war council. We were all busy talking over what to do and how to find the location of our arch enemy, Lord Doom. Reports from all sectors came up empty. We needed to find out what the fiend was up to—and how to defeat him—as well as to defeat the entity he served.

Zaor was there, Aron the Eldest, and King Shamar as well, Konor king of the Blues of Vognar had come over from the faraway western continent, even General Zod, commander of the Blue Kortas had attended to put forth his own plan urging instant harsh military action; and of course Admiral of the fleet, Quarto-Zar was in attendance. We had come up with theory and plan, after theory and plan, but so far nothing would give us an inkling of where Lord Doom was located, or what he might be up to. He was certainly up to something that I knew would place us in deadly danger. Doom's mind powers were substantial—no doubt augmented by those of his master, the alien entity he served. Even a mind master of the power of Aron the Eldest could not discover what Doom was up to. It was evident we were desperate and needed additional help—but where would we be able to get that help?

"We are being blocked," was all Lord Aron reported to us in a dull voice of quiet exasperation. "It is most annoying and most effective."

It was wily Ras-noor, a protégé of my deceased old friend Tar-gool, who delivered to us the true goods on the matter—and it was grim news indeed.

"Jon Kirk, may I speak?"

"Ras-noor, my old friend, come forward. You have news you wish to report to the War Council?" I asked the old science master. He was in attendance with leaders of his teams in all the various fields of the sciences. These were now the greatest scientific minds on Ares, and Ras-noor led them and mentored them so as to make sure they would become the great scientific leaders that we would need in the future. They were the future of science on Ares and throughout the empire.

"Yes, My Emperor, but perhaps…?"

"No, you may speak freely here, we are all on the same team with the same objectives."

Ras-noor nodded, thought for a moment and then began, "I have reason to believe that we are under attack at this very moment, Jon Kirk. However, the enemy is not using anything so conventional as warships from outer space or armies of warriors to land on our planets to attack us. Lord Doom has somehow managed the ability to harness a small moon, a dead black moon of exceptional heavy mass. It is far away now, but he is hurling it toward Ares at this very moment. That is why, I believe, Lord Doom has not attacked us with his Enemy Empire fleet, he is using their energy rays and power beams to control the direction of this black moon—putting it on a collision course with Ares."

There was utter silence at this news and then turmoil growing among everyone in the chamber. Loud talk, questions that grew into more frantic words that were tinged with fear. How could this happen? How soon until the moon hit Ares? What would the results be of such a collision? I could feel the panic growing. I knew reason among many there upon this subject would not last long, and I looked to Gorm, who only nodded back to me with a grim wary smile.

"Order! All of you! I say order!" Gorm of the Gorms shouted the demand in his resounding voice that rang throughout that chamber as he pounded his enormous battle ax upon the heavy table to lend fierce emphasis to his thunderous words. That certainly got every-one's attention and most all there soon became quiet and listened to what was to be said next by the huge alien warrior who was forcefully exerting his authority over everyone in that huge chamber. "Order! Your Emperor demands it!"

There was utter quiet now for a telling moment, a stark stillness, then some of the leaders of the empire voiced their views and concerns.

"This is terrible news!" Konor of the Blues of Vognar stated showing obvious distress and concern for his people who lived on the other side of the planet. "What can we do?"

"Such a collision will surely destroy Ares," Admiral Quarto-Zar stated with calm military certainty. "We must do something to forestall this at once."

It was certainly the understatement of the year. My new Winged man friend did not need to tell me that. I realized at once the imminent danger to Ares only too well. I could just not believe that Doom would be able to achieve such a thing as to precisely direct a moon across the billions of miles of interstellar space to collide with Ares. I could not believe it—but I realized it just might be possible. That shook me as it did all those who heard about it.

I looked at Ras-noor carefully, "Are you certain of your facts?"

"Yes, Jon Kirk, we are certain of the facts. The science of the thing makes it possible. The black moon was brought from very far away—perhaps even outside of our galaxy. It is an incredibly heavy metal moon, and Lord Doom's fleet of warships is hidden behind it. I believe the incredible metal mass of the moon makes him and his fleet undetectable to even our most sensitive scientific instruments and sensors, and it may even obstruct the mental powers of the Keven mind masters."

I saw Lord Aron nod his head sadly in agreement at the disclosure of this information. "If what Ras-noor says is true, Jon Kirk, then this may be why my Keven mind masters, even with Lord Kneth's aid, have been unable to locate Lord Doom and his fleet."

"Well, that is a moot point at this time. We certainly know now where Doom and his fleet are! And we know what he is up to! What I need to know now, is what can we do about it? How do we stop him?" I asked seeking bold swift action. I was open for suggestions. Should we just explode the moon? I wondered, was it even possible? I feared nothing was ever so simple as it seemed.

I received a plethora of answers and plans to my question, but the gist of the replies of all the men and women in that chamber pointed me in the direction of what I had already decided to do. I knew now that I had to take our fleet and meet the black moon, and out there in the dark void of space, seek battle to destroy Lord Doom and his fleet—and then destroy that black moon before it ever came near Ares. It seemed like the proper plan, but I knew it could be an impossible task as the enemy fleet would fight us every step of the way and we knew they outnumbered us by at least double the amount of ships. That this also might be some kind of trap seemed a foregone conclusion, but I knew we had no choice now. We had to go out and meet this new threat and defeat it.

I told my thoughts on the matter to my ministers and advisors and they all agreed that such action seemed the only proper way open to us. They strongly advised we act quickly before the black moon and Doom's fleet approached too close to Ares. I agreed, but was still wary that this might be some kind of feint or trap, but there seemed nothing else to do but move on the threat.

"So be it!" I ordered firmly. "Admiral Quarto-Zar, prepare your fleet immediately. Zaor you will accompany me."

"Of course, My Emperor."

I looked at the people in that room, nodded. "Thank you all. Now let us not waste any more time, every moment that passes means the black moon is moving closer to Ares. We all know what that means."

"How long do we have before the collision with Ares takes place, Ras-noor?" Aron the Eldest asked our science maven.

"One week, My Lord," the old scientist replied.

"That is good, then we have some time," Lord Kneth chimed in.

"Yet it may not be enough time," Ras-noor cautioned.

"Then let us be off!" I ordered firmly, my generals and the leaders of the empire moved with busy eagerness. I told them all, "Sahn-jor will remain here in command. Do what you can, my friend. Aron the Eldest and the Kevens, with Lord Kneth will remain here with Ras-noor and his people as well. All of you do what you can to protect Ares, my friends, find a way, for if we fail…"

I did not need to finish that sentence.

"Yes, My Emperor," King Shamar and Lord Aron replied together.

Sahn-jor looked grim but nodded.

I looked at all three men, my good friends, and my hand firmly grasped their shoulders, "See if you can come up with something—anything—for I have a fear that this mission may be nothing more than a trap. Lord Doom is a devious and cunning villain and stopping him may not be as simple as I would like to believe. Nor as it might appear."

"Yes, My Emperor," Lord Aron replied, giving me a knowing smile. Then in a low whisper he said, "Nothing is ever as it seems, but do not despair."

"No I shall not despair, at least not yet," I told him in a low tone. Then I spoke up in a stronger voice, "Never!"

The old Keven mind master gave me another slight smile. It was a good sign to see him showing some outward manifestation of hope at my words. Hope was something that seemed in short supply among us these days.

"We will not let you down, Jon Kirk," Sahn-jor told me in a determined voice. I thanked my old friend, then looked to my lovely Sirah, and little Alun.

"And now, to my wife and son, I must see them and say my farewells," I said, preparing to leave for our private living quarters elsewhere in the palace, but I was surprised to see standing suddenly before me—appearing as if by magic—my beloved wife Sirah, and she was with our young son, Alun. They stood before me glowing with smiles and it delighted me to see them. After all, they were what I was fighting for. They were what life meant to me now.

"I heard the news, Jon Kirk," Sirah told me as she rushed into my arms and we kissed and hugged each other fiercely. Little Alun joined us and the three of us held each other tightly for a long wonderful moment that I wished would last forever, but was over far too soon. I had to break the embrace. I had work to do now.

"I love you," I told her in a husky tone.

"I know," Sirah replied with pursed moist lips, "and I love you, Jon Kirk, My Emperor. Please come back to me—to us."

"I will, Sirah, and you little Alun, I will," I said firmly, or at least I would do everything that I could to make that happen. There was nothing I wanted more in life, but I had a dangerous mission to perform now, a deadly dangerous mission and a world to save. I said my farewells to my darling wife and son, as I watched my friend Zaor do the same with his own wife, the lovely Manalia. I waited, giving them a few more precious private moments together, knowing these might be the last moments they had this side of life.

Quarto-Zar, the huge Winged-man Admiral of our fleet, stood beside me patiently waiting. Finally he whispered in his hoarse fierce rasping voice, "Jon Kirk, I have already alerted the fleet, the ships and their crews stand by ready, waiting. We should go now."

I nodded, he was right, of course. "Zaor, we need to go. Let us be off!"

Zaor kissed his wife once more in fond farewell.

Sirah broke down and cried as she flung herself at me, her arms wrapped around my neck and her lips smothering my own. I was conscious of my small son, Alun, wrapping his arms tightly around my legs in an effort to stop me from leaving, but I was a man with a job to do. And while I was the emperor, I was also a warrior and a fighting man. A fighting man who knew I might never see my lovely wife and young son again. They knew they might never see me again either. It was the harsh reality of the situation of a fighting man whenever going into battle. I softly and carefully dislodged Sirah and Alun from me, kissing each of them fondly, and then said, "I must be off now."

"Of course," Sirah said holding back her tears and standing tall and proud with little Alun at her side. "Good hunting, My Emperor."

"Yes, to good hunting, and to victory!" I replied voicing the standard Ares warrior response. Then I quickly left the huge audience chamber with Zaor and Quarto-Zar, my admiral and my general at my side. We were quickly escorted to a waiting flier that would take us up to our warships that were now held in stationary Ares orbit.

CHAPTER 11

The Battle at the Black Moon

Our fleet had been traveling through the vast darkness of outer space for three long days. In all that time I knew the black moon was getting closer to Ares. It was coming towards us—as we were coming towards it—then it would pass us, and head on to Ares.

The ships of the Sindalki that were now a part of our fleet, augmented with crew possessing Keven mind powers, as well as powered by Ancient Ares super-science, moved quickly through the great void. Our warships shot through the vast area of Known Space for three days, but soon we would approach the black moon that was rushing on a collision course with Ares—and we had to stop it. Somehow.

"You can see it now," Quarto-Zar told me in careful warning.

I saw it then. I was standing upon the bridge of the admiral's flagship, *Valladont*, which in the Zar language means 'Battle Ready'. I thought it to be a fine name for a deadly warship and I hoped the name would prove true—but I put that thought out of my mind as my eyes locked upon the black moon now fully appearing on the front view screens of the ship's bridge. It was just now coming into view and I was immediately astonished at seeing it. It was an incredible sight.

It was an enormous dark moon, about the size of Earth's own, which remembrance brought my grim thoughts back to the destruction of the Earth and all her people by Lord Doom. This moon however, was massive and darkly sinister for it was made of the most weighty of heavy metals. It's mass was large but its incredible gravity force was terrific. It gave off an aura of light around it that seemed to distort the very space it passed through. I wondered what the metal was that it was composed of. Lead, or something surely just as heavy, if not more so. It was simply so massive and so heavy, it seemed to distort the very space it passed through. I wondered if it had even originated from our galaxy at all. It also had that most strange and peculiar aura to it which had me wondering. What did that strange aura mean? The huge moon looked deadly, and it was certainly being used as a most deadly weapon. Lord Doom was going to use the moon to destroy Ares, and all the people I knew who lived there, everything I held dear in my life. That would not happen if I could help it! It could *not* happen! I vowed my revenge! I also knew one other thing now. Lord Doom certainly was here, somewhere aboard one of these enemy warships, somewhere in that vast enemy fleet, unseen at the moment, protected behind the black moon. Doom was here! The Sindalki lord was obviously directing the projectile with the beam weapons of the ships of his fleet, even as the small planetoid shielded his warships from our own weapons and sensors.

"Can you see the enemy fleet?" I asked Quarto, my Zaran admiral.

"They are there, My Emperor, over one hundred vessels, all Enemy Empire design. However, this is only a small part of the vast Enemy Empire fleet. We know of ten times this number of enemy warships in total. Where are all the others? We have determined that they possess over one thousand warships in their massive fleet."

"Then where are those other ships?" I asked my admiral.

"Not known at this time, My Emperor," Quarto replied with a shake of his massive black Zaran wings. "Perhaps the Kin-Ty-Roo is holding the majority of the fleet back for protection? Or a flank attack? Or some other purpose?"

I nodded, or a trap of some kind, but I could not worry about those other ships now. They were not here. We had enough of a problem with this smaller fleet of just one hundred Enemy Empire warships that were here—so as long as the rest of the enemy fleet did not appear, I was not going to worry about them for now. If they did not show up—and they were nowhere to be seen—then maybe we could put up a decent fight and come out of this with our hides intact. A long shot, but it was worth a try. I knew those many hundreds of enemy warships would have to be dealt with, but later. However, if they did appear now, we were in big trouble. I had a feeling we were being drawn into some kind of a trap or sly feint. The whereabouts of the missing Enemy Empire ships had me concerned and stumped, and quite fearful. Where were they? If the rest of the enemy fleet appeared here, that would be the end of us all. Would they turn up when we least expected them? There was just no way to know.

Admiral Quarto spoke up giving me the current scenario, "We are surely outnumbered but we can hit them before they know we are here *if* we move quickly. Their ships are packed very closely behind the black moon, so tightly that their sensor devices will not pick us up right away. They can not, as yet, get through our jamming, and the heavy metal of the moon interferes with their sensors—as it does so with our own. The aura it emits may also block sensors. I assume it also interferes with Lord Doom's mind powers in some manner. If we hit the enemy hard now, we may dislodge them from their posi tion of safety behind the black moon. Then we can cut out individual vessels and destroy them—or we will at least have a better chance to destroy some of them."

That sounded like a hopeful plan, but I knew what that meant, for it meant only a slim chance for us to win in any ship-to-ship space battle. However, my main thoughts were on the black moon and Ares just then.

"Can we somehow explode that damn thing?" I asked my admiral hopefully. "I want that moon taken out before it gets anywhere near Ares."

"Exploding the moon out here in deep space so far away from Ares would cause no damage to any inhabited world and would surely settle the danger once and for all." Zaor added hopefully.

"Yes, perhaps, but we must defeat Doom's fleet first, before we can concentrate upon the moon, My General, My Emperor," Quarto-Zar replied in a serious tone to our questions. He explained once more, "The fleet protects the moon with shielding we can not penetrate. We must destroy the fleet first, so that then we can get at the moon."

"Of course," I replied feeling a bit rebuffed by the extent and hopelessness of the problem confronting us.

Zaor queried the admiral, "I still say why not just explode the black moon here and now? You have massively powerful weapons. There must be some way to do it."

Quarto-Zar smiled grimly but he did not take offense by my general's question. His great dark leathery face, red piercing eyes,

Winged-man stance seemed to soften, as he said, "Because My General, Lord Doom's fleet protects the moon with their shielding as I have already told you. The moon and the fleet are held together in some kind of energy field we can not break. That is also the reason they have not discovered us yet. But time is running out, and as we draw closer, they will soon become aware of us. Then a decision must be made."

Zaor fumed in apparent frustration but did not take Quarto's words as an insult. They were not meant to be, I was sure. And so was Zaor.

"Then attack now, Quarto!" I ordered quickly. "Send our ships directly at the black moon and then up and around behind it to fire upon Doom's fleet from the rear in a surprise attack. We can outflank them."

"Yes, My Emperor, that seems to be our only chance. Anticipating your plan, I have already given the order for our ships to form up."

I looked carefully at my fleet admiral and allowed a wry smile, the huge Zaran Winged-man returned to me a most fierce warlike grin. He had named his flagship *Valladont*, which meant *Battle Ready* in Zaran, and it seemed most apropos now. At least I hoped so.

CHAPTER 12

Boarder's Away!

The Battle of the Black Moon proved to be an epic space fight that will go down in the annals of galactic warfare throughout the many worlds encompassing the Known Universe. One hundred warships of the Enemy Empire fleet led by Lord Karlath Doom—evil surrogate of the entity known as the Kin-Ty-Roo—were attacked in a rapid flanking surprise maneuver by more than fifty of our own massive space faring warships. These were Admiral Quarto-Zar's surviving warships, formerly in the service of the Secret Empire of the dead Sindalki race. Now they and their crews were fighting for us and Ares in a battle of revenge and survival.

Of course, our ships went to invisibility right away, but just as soon as we did this, the ships of the enemy fleet did likewise. They had the same forces and powers at their disposal as we did. In essence, and because of this, the power of invisibility proved useless once again for both sides—sensors enabled both sides to easily 'see' each other's ships even though they were not able to be seen visibly by the naked eye. It did not matter now. Invisibility was a moot factor in this war and quite useless. Other modes of battle had to be enacted.

The ships of both fleets met in a slamming swarm of whirling chaos, coming at each other in instantaneous paths of incredible speed, shooting deadly beams of unimaginable force and power at each other that enveloped them in bright light and blinding fire. The very universe itself seemed to be alive with bright flares and inconceivable destruction on a massive scale. Warships were hit, hit again, and battered so hard that weakened shields on some vessels finally gave out. Hulls were dented and slammed, and sometimes would break and burst open. When that happened the luckless ship, and those aboard her, would find themselves helpless in a vessel that would a moment later become an incredible incandescent explosion of blinding brilliance. Then it was gone.

Most of the ships came at each other in small groups, or even fighting in individual battles. It reminded me much of the ancient aerial dogfights I had heard tell of long ago back upon Earth in World War I—the so-called 'war to end all wars', as it had been called back on my beloved lost home planet. Ship fought against ship, beams of force and energy swarmed over shields, overwhelmed them, and then sometimes tore into the metal hulls and walls to burst open the vessel in an explosion of unimaginable incandescent chaos. Lifeless bodies of crew members were flung willy-nilly out into the darkness of open space, most were unsuited, unprotected. They floated or shot forward on some unknown trajectory without any destination from the chaos of battle damage to their ship. It was an atrocity—and still both sides fought on ever harder. In this form of battle there was no substitute for victory.

I was growing anxious knowing that my supreme enemy was here, somewhere on one of these ships. I wanted Lord Doom! I made a plan with Admiral Quarto and talked it over with Zaor and my huge warrior-friend, Gorm. I told them my plan. They were all for it. They already had their warriors gathering and preparing for action.

I told them, "We can not transport our troops into the enemy ships, we do not have that technology, but Admiral, if you can get this ship close enough to an Enemy Empire ship, we can cut our way inside through their shielding and then the hull, and if so, then we can board it. Then our warriors can fight to take control of that ship. Can you get us in that close?"

"Yes, Jon Kirk, but you will be risking much to invade an enemy warship in such a manner," Quarto said his face tense with dire warning. I could see that he saw the action as nothing but a suicide run. I did not think so, or at least I hoped it would not prove to be so.

"We are game. All I need to know is if the air on the enemy ships are breathable for me and my men."

"Yes, it is, My Emperor, all vessels in both fleets use a similar mixture of breathable air," Quarto said with a grim smile. "Your men will not need any special breathing devices."

"Good, then Zaor, Gorm, tell your men to get ready for action!"

"They are ready and waiting!" Zaor replied with gusto.

"Action is good!" Gorm growled with a grim smile as he hefted his huge battle ax in anticipatory readiness. He was always eager for a fight.

Zaor looked at me and just smiled. He was waiting impatiently, another bold warrior who was ever ready for action.

"Then let's go!" I shouted. My boarding party was armed and ready. They had been prepared for just such an action and were looking forward to close battle with the enemy. They were even hungry for it. As was I. Whatever damage we could inflict upon Doom's fleet, on his ships, on his crews, would be worthwhile. And who knew, perhaps I might even come upon Lord Doom himself. I lived for such an eventuality.

"Boarder's ready!" I barked the sharp command to get things going.

A hundred heads silently nodded, grunted eager shouts and stark war cries. These were serious warriors holding their weapons ready with rapt anticipation. Swords, pikes, spears, axes, death ray pistols and projectile rifles were all out and ready for use. Each one of my fighters set his personal body shield set on, which we knew might offer some protection from some enemy weapons—but never all of them.

Admiral Quarto deftly brought his ship broadside to an Enemy Empire warship. The two warships touched, clanged together, force fields held the ships together for the brief moments we would need. The sector of shielding of the enemy vessel we targeted was quickly brought down, then the hull of the enemy vessel was quickly breached with ray weapons. Now the opening was made for an airlock that would be our pathway into the enemy vessel. I had recently led spaceship boarding parties into Enemy Empire warships, so I knew what had to be done to ensure victory. The crews of our enemy were not trained to repel boarders in this manner, and in fact, they never considered they could be boarded and defeated in this type of action. It was a most low-tech solution to a high-tec space battle. But it often proved effective, especially when the enemy was not anticipating such an attack and was not trained on how to repel a boarding party. I only hoped the enemy had not augmented their training since our last battle.

"Let's go! Follow me!" I barked as I ran into the bowels of the enemy warship, followed by a hundred grim heavily armed warriors furious to bring revenge and bloody death to the defenders. We went into the enemy ship like a pack of screaming banshees.

We hit their defensive line hard and took down all who stood before us. The enemy crews, and their few Marines, were no match for Gorm and Zaor, and myself—and the hundred bold warriors we led into the enemy vessel. We took down that first line of defense fairly quickly, with no injuries to our side. Then we moved deeper inside the ship, taking deck after deck, moving inexorably towards the bridge, where we would take full control of the vessel. For I had a plan. I had a plan to take this ship and then turn its weapons against Lord Doom's other ships. I knew that such an action would cause utter chaos within the enemy fleet. That chaos could stall or even halt their attack. It would surely set their fleet in total disarray and maybe even set them at each other's throats, if I was lucky. The fog of battle could cause such chaos, and I was doing all I could to egg on that chaos among the enemy.

In the meantime, I fought madly, pushing my attack and taking down every enemy defender I came across. Using my sword, along with a death ray pistol, I cut down a dozen of the enemy crewmen who came at us with their own deadly weapons. Gorm of the Gorms wielded his massive battle ax in a whirling fury that cut down entire swaths of the enemy defenders. They learned to move away from him and his deadly weapon very quickly. And stay away! Meanwhile Zaor, and a group with him pushed forward into the enemy ranks and hit them so hard that soon the defenders had apparently had enough. I saw them throw down their weapons in abject defeat. They now signaled surrender.

The fight to take the ship had been furious and bloody but it was over now. Admiral Quarto had already disengaged his warship from this one. Now we were on our own. I had control of an enemy warship.

At this moment my real battle plan went into operation as I ordered the enemy captain to set his ship's weapons upon the ships of his own fleet. I ordered the captain to deftly maneuver his vessel between two Enemy Empire warships, and then told him to open fire upon both unwary warships with all weapons. Once he did so, it caused devastating results. The two Enemy Empire ships were unaware of our new status and did not fight back, both quickly exploded into monumental destructive chaos.

A cheer rang out upon the bridge among the members of my boarding party.

"So far so good!" I shouted, to the roar of approval of my men clustered upon the bridge. Gorm loved the bright explosions of the enemy ships. Zaor just smiled, pointing to another enemy ship that was now coming into range to investigate.

"It is a big one, Jon Kirk!" Zaor shouted out in anticipation. "A battleship!"

"Good, then we take that one next!"

I saw the huge ship and nodded, and so ordered the enemy captain to make for it, and he did as he was instructed. The enemy captain did as he was told because Gorm was holding him in a most uncomfortable manner and convincing him with dire personal threats of what would happen should he not obey my orders exactly as they were given. As the enemy captain was another *consignat*—impressed fighter—he was not all that hard set on dying for Lord Doom. So he quickly did as he was told.

The next Enemy Empire warship now came in closer. The battleship's massive array of guns was now trained upon us. That told me all I needed to know. I knew that the jig was up, this enemy captain had figured out that our ship had been taken over—so he brought his battleship closer in with guns blazing. I ordered our captain to do likewise and the two warships stood face to face slugging it out with all kinds of energy and beam weapons. The firepower was furious. The ships hitting each other with devastating energy beams and projectiles. We were getting the worst of the situation. While we were inflicting terrible damage upon the enemy battleship, they were giving as good as they got—and quite a bit more. They were crippling our vessel. I knew that it was but a matter of time before both ships would be destroyed, but we would go down first. So be it! I instructed our weapons to keep firing upon the enemy until the last moment. Then, once we reached the point of no return, which I knew must come soon, I gave the final command. We had done all that was possible.

"Abandon ship!" I ordered in a loud firm voice tinged with regret. Then to my men, "Get the prisoners and our crew to the lifeboats right away! Get out of here now! Abandon ship!"

We quickly left our conquered ship, our lifeboats away and safe, just before the Enemy Empire battleship blew it out of existence.

The ship we had taken control of was gone now, but we had all made our way safely back to Quarto's nearby flagship aboard the smaller lifeboats. Once we were back aboard Quarto's flagship, and the enemy prisoners taken away, I looked over at my men, at Zaor, Gorm, and all the others and they gave me a wild cheer. We had done it!

"I guess that showed them!" Gorm barked in a wild voice of glorious victory.

"Now let's do it again!" Zaor barked out flush with the fury of battle and victory.

"Yes, how about we do it again!" I shouted back to him with a wild grin. Then I ordered, "Boarders get ready! Admiral find us another target on the other side of the enemy fleet. A ship that may not have heard the news about us yet. Then let's board another one!"

That got them all fired up for more action. The men cheered and followed me to a part of our flagship where we could access the airlock after we had pulled close to an enemy ship's hull, take down that section of their shields, then open a breach in the hull, and then board the enemy ship. Admiral Quarto seemed to have found us another perfect target. A heavy cruiser that bristled with weapons. Our ship moved in fast.

Once again I led the boarding party, and we swarmed into another Enemy Empire warship. The enemy crew never knew what hit them. This time the fight was over even faster than previously and we took control of the ship rather quickly. Then I saw to it that the enemy's heavy cruiser trained its weapons to fire upon the ships of its own fleet. It did so with amazing results. The action caused devastating chaos among ships of the enemy fleet. It was glorious to see. The effect upon Lord Doom's fleet must have been stunning—not a lot of actual damage, for we only lightly damaged a few ships this way—but shields failed and the chaos and fear we caused made the impact of our actions ten times worse than they really were. It was all worth it—if we could do it and get away with it alive.

That day I led boarding parties that ended up taking two more Enemy Empire warships in this manner, and for a while it put the enemy fleet into total chaos. However, even though we were victorious and won control of two of their warships—using them to fire their weapons upon five others of their own warships, and exploding one of them into horrific incandescence—I realized that this approach to fighting Doom's fleet would take too long and would never lead to victory. And the enemy was getting wise to this tactic and preparing for us.

Another approach was needed.

And still the black moon hurled towards Ares.

CHAPTER 13

The Battle Continues

There is no sound in space—thank God—for the explosions were simply terrible and the sounds of those explosions had they appeared upon any planetary surface would have been incredibly brutal. Loud enough to knock out a man's hearing—or unnerve his very mind. As it was, the bright incandescent light pounded the eyes and shook the minds of everyone in the crews on the ships of both fleets.

The Battle of the Black Moon raged on for many more hours and from time to time ships from both sides struck killing blows that sent their opponent vessel down into fiery incandescent death. Initially, the two sides had seemed to be fairly evenly matched since we had taken advantage of the aspect of surprise that had been on our side at the beginning, but that did not last long and I could see that we were not winning as time went on. We could not win. We simply did not have the numbers. What's more important, I noticed that no matter what we did we were not able to explode the black moon, or even stop its trajectory, and that after all, was our main mission. This had me dreadfully concerned, and I felt growing alarm as I watched the battle progress around me—even as the black moon moved un-molested upon its dreadful course to destroy the world and people I loved. It seemed unstoppable.

"I still do not understand why we can not blast that damnable moon into a billion lumps of rock right now?" Zaor asked the admiral in frustration once again, as if some other answer might make itself known from the one he had heard explained to him twice before. Nothing had changed. His anger was great and his sheer frustration even greater. He could not accept that we were helpless to stop the black moon. I knew he feared for his mate Manalia, back upon Ares.

I also wondered if there was some way to explode the black moon, but I was afraid that I knew the answer only too well to that question. It had already been answered by the Admiral, and since that time, nothing much had changed in our ability to attain that which we wanted to do.

The big Zaran Winged-man looked at me sadly. "Jon Kirk, I know how you and Lord Zaor feel, but there is still some manner of shield or shield-like power that protects the black moon from our weapons. Even now. Our few victories mean nothing in the larger scope of this battle. I am sorry. We can not destroy it. We also can not go around it any longer. We can not place our ships in a position so our scientists can aim our weapons to outflank the cover posed by the enemy shielding."

I nodded. "I know that, Quarto."

"However, there is something that we have been able to learn. It appears this shielding is no longer coming from the enemy fleet's own shields, as we first thought. There is some other power that seems to be protecting the black moon," the admiral told us.

"Yes, it has to be. Lord Doom's mind power, I am sure," I stated in growing frustration, for I was sure of that fact now, and knew that the monster that I loathed and feared was behind all this madness.

"Yes, that could be, perhaps that is true, for his own dark mind power is substantial, he is a mind master of the first order, My Emperor," Quarto-Zar stated with a nod of his huge winged head. Then he added grimly, "Or perhaps, Jon Kirk, it is coming from some other source."

"The Kin-Ty-Roo?" I asked carefully in a thick tone. If this was true, this was not good news. Thus far the alien entity had not shown itself in any apparent outward manifestation, allowing its surrogates and minions like Doom to do the actual dirty work. I had not thought the alien entity would involve itself in Doom's battle here. Perhaps I was wrong?

"That may be the situation, Jon Kirk," the admiral replied, bowing his head with a long look of regret. "Lord Doom may be drawing power from the entity for his action here."

"Then his fleet and the black moon being out here were definitely set as a trap for us," I stated with a shake of my head, growing more concerned, knowing such a trap was not only possible but probable now. If that was true then victory might be impossible for us to achieve. I grew grim. Something needed to be done. I needed a game changer.

I looked closely at my admiral. He slowly walked closer to me.

"Perhaps it is a trap, but I can not see why that would be so, Jon Kirk. If the black moon hits Ares it will kill all life on that world—so why should the Sindalki lord fight a battle here and jeopardize his fleet against our own?" Quarto asked, ever the pragmatic commander. "It does not make sense to me."

"He is not jeopardizing his fleet. This must have been a trap, to tempt us out here where he can destroy our fleet. Then he will send the black moon on its way to continue on a collision course with Ares. Doom seeks to kill two birds with one stone, our fleet and Ares," I said, using another of my so-called 'quaint Earthly sayings' as Zaor was so fond of calling them, but all there fully understood the meaning behind my words. Then I continued, "But our fleet might yet escape. Doom wants our fleet defeated, but he also wants me as well. I am sure now that he wants me pretty bad. Perhaps I can use that hatred to put a crimp in his plan? We must defeat or delay this fleet, and then find some way to explode the black moon before it gets near Ares."

"There is something else, Jon Kirk, that we should consider," Zaor said now in a quiet tone. "Lord Doom may be doing this on his own. He may have gone rogue. You well know the animus he feels towards you, it may be blocking out his better sense of mission, or his obidience to his master, the alien entity. He may even be doing this action on his own, *despite* his master's knowledge or wishes."

I looked sharply at Zaor, "I find that improbable. I do not think so, Zaor, it seems impossible—but then again Doom has his own twisted reasons, so who can say for certain."

"If this is true, then Doom's fight here may not be sanctioned by his master, or is being done without the full knowledge—or not under the order—of the Kin-Ty-Roo. It would not be the first time that a minion has gone over the head of a master in an action he took for personal reasons," Zaor added thoughtfully.

"Personal reasons, yes, that may be the key, Jon Kirk," Gorm of the Gorms growled.

I nodded, it seemed possible, but why? Was Doom's hatred of me that deep and malignant? Was he that insane to defy even the will of his master the Kin-Ty-Roo? Yes, the more I thought about it, I had to admit, perhaps he was.

Admiral Quarto-Zar spoke up, "My Emperor, we are trying our best to fight off the attackers. We are trying to break the power of the shield they have formulated around the black moon. I have my best technicians and scientists working on that now. Our ships are putting up a valiant fight against Doom's fleet, but I fear we can not win this outcome with our present mode of action. A new plan is needed. Presently we are in a precarious stalemate, but that is a temporary situation, for I am sure the tide will turn against us soon. We have done much damage to the enemy and destroyed some of their ships, but we are still seriously outnumbered and we have incurred many damaged and destroyed ships of our own."

"Yes, I know, and…?" I asked carefully with some hesitation.

Admiral Quarto-Zar did not reply right away, but looked at me carefully.

"Quarto, what is on your mind?" I asked firmly, for I could see something was disturbing the large winged creature and this was most unusual.

"I feel we must protect the fleet, at all cost, My Lord. We must save it from destruction," he said firmly, meaningfully. I knew just what that meant.

I nodded, of course, I could see the odds were against us, and I could read the way the battle was going. Our brave crews and warships were outnumbered and losing the fight. If we continued in this mode of operation we would have no ships left to fight with.

I spoke up firmly, "Admiral, please order an immediate withdrawal of our fleet."

"Yes, My Emperor," Quarto replied showing sad resignation, but offering a positive nod of his huge Zaran head "A wise decision."

"We may have put up a brave fight and done the enemy some damage, but we would have lost the battle and our entire fleet if we continue the fight against them head-on for too much longer—and that means losing the war," Zaor spoke to me in a sad whisper. "I am sorry, Jon Kirk."

"So am I," I whispered holding back a feeling of abject resignation. Was this the road to defeat I had feared for so long?

"But take heed, my friend, all is not lost," Zaor responded with a grim smile.

I took his words to heart. I was resolved to find a way out of this enigma and still grasp the victory we needed. I gritted my teeth. This was the time for a game changer and I think I had an idea in that respect.

"I still live, Zaor! You still live! We will find a way around this!" I told him with powerful determination and a deep well of hope. I would not allow defeat to overcome our mission or hinder our thoughts from the victory we deserved.

The warships of our fleet immediately broke contact with the Enemy Empire fleet and quickly moved off. Now Ares was less guarded from an attack by our enemy, save for the platform projectors Ras-noor had placed upon the mountains of the planet. Meanwhile, Doom's fleet and the black moon were still rushing headlong and unstoppable upon their deadly course, surging towards Ares unmolested.

I fumed in rage and frustration at the dire situation we now found ourselves in. This truly seemed to be my darkest hour. I thought of my beloved Sirah, and little Alun, and all the people of Ares—even as I still mourned the Earth and all the people who had lived and loved there. Doom had to be stopped. There had to be a way.

"Perhaps we can not beat his fleet in a set battle," I told my admiral, "but we can try to delay them, and certainly harass them?"

"How so, Jon Kirk?" Quarto asked attentively with a snarl or a smile, ready to grasp at any plan that might bring us some advantage in this fight.

"We harry them, harass them, take our fleet to the outer fringes of their own, follow behind them at a discrete distance, then come up behind them and attack. We have our ships concentrate all fire power to pick off one enemy ship at a time. This might further reduce their numbers somewhat, and anything to reduce his force is acceptable. I do not think Doom will go off mission to come after us with his full force if we do that. He will see an occasional single ship lost as an acceptable cost of battle. He will not want to interfere with his main mission, which is transporting the black moon to Ares. If so, then we can do some more damage to his fleet. Whatever we can do is worth it. He wants to deliver the black moon to Ares, and he will stop at nothing to do that, but we shall make it as costly as possible for him to accomplish that goal. And who knows, perhaps we can whittle his force down enough so that by the time he gets to Ares, we can take more of his ships out in an all-out attack? Can we do that, Admiral?"

"Perhaps. At least we can try. Yes, I believe we can do something along those lines. Communications officer, give the new plans I have just set on my comm to all our ships and have our fleet rendezvous behind the Enemy Empire fleet. Once on station, on my order, we will proceed to target and concentrate our fire, all weapons from all ships upon a single targeted enemy ship. I will mark the coordinates."

I nodded, feeling some hope at hearing these orders being given.

Zaor gave me a reassuring grin.

Gorm just looked at his battle axe lovingly, anticipating future action.

I thought about what we were doing now. I hoped at least this might buy us some time. It would certainly get Doom's attention and cause him to send out ships to confront us—but not his entire fleet. And that bothered me. No matter what action we took now, it would not be enough and it could not stop Doom's plan. In truth, we were only an annoyance to him now. In the meantime the black moon still inexorably moved onward towards Ares without being stopped. That had me most fearful. If this plan of action worked, Doom would have a weaker force as time passed and he got closer to Ares, but I held little hope that it might mean we had a better chance to get in there and bust him up—kill his fleet or destroy the black moon. I had little real hope. It knew I was playing a dangerous game and time was running out, but this seemed the only game in town for us now.

And then another thought came into my mind. I took a minute to roll it around in my consciousness to see if it might work. It seemed crazy. Perhaps even foolish. I was not quite sure about it, but it seemed that it might give me a chance. I was all about taking chances.

The battle raged on. Our warships had now taken out one more of the enemy warships, and little by little, we were determined to diminish the number of the ships in Doom's fleet. So far one of his prize warships had been destroyed, and one more had been seriously damaged. It limped along with the enemy fleet protected by sister ships. If we continued to apply the right pressure, this ship also could be gone soon. But the enemy fleet was still massive, Lord Doom still had many serviceable ships, many more than he needed. The black moon was still protected by some type of shield we could not penetrate. The shielding seemed to be something that did not originate from any scientific device on any of Lord Doom's ships, or so our fleet scientists told us.

CHAPTER 14

Jon Kirk's Plan

"We know what it might be," I stated to the officers around me upon the bridge of our flagship. This was not science any of us there knew much about. "It is certainly some manifestation of super mind power that we can not stop. Doom is using some type of Sindalki mental power or magic to shield the black moon—or he has tapped into some type of power from the Kin-Ty-Roo. I am sure that were Lord Kneth here he would know for sure. How Doom is doing this is beyond me, but as long as he can protect the black moon, we can not destroy it. And we must destroy it soon. I know what I must do now. I must take the battle to Doom himself."

"Yes, I am afraid you are correct, Jon Kirk, you must take the battle to Doom yourself. You must battle him one-on-one, find some manner to get onto his flagship, and then slay him! Meet him on the Physical Plane in personal battle," Zaor stated boldly. He was serious and I agreed, but I looked at him with a sly nod of my head. He knew he had something there, but it was easier said than done. However, just such an action had been my idea for a while now and I thought that it could work—but I did not know if I would ever get the opportunity to try my idea—or how to make it work. Now it appeared we had no other alternatives—though I wondered how I was to achieve my plan.

"Slay him, of course—but that would mean for me to slay him yet *again!* You forget, Zaor, I already have killed the beast in a sword fight but a scant few days ago on Ares. Then he regenerated. He came back to life. It seems he can not be killed," I told my friend feeling the hopelessness of the situation almost overwhelm me.

"Anyone or anything can be killed, Jon Kirk," Zaor said with the absolute certitude of the warrior. "Even Lord Doom."

"But I have already killed him once!" I replied thoughtfully, for this was a most perplexing problem. I looked to my friend carefully.

Zaor just grinned at me, "So kill him again, but this time make sure it lasts forever!"

I looked at my old friend and gave him a firm nod of agreement. Zaor was right of course. His words spoke to my very heart as coming from the true soul of a valiant warrior, a fighting man, and I realized that as a fighting man myself, this battle would never be over until I won it myself and killed Lord Doom! Forever!

I looked over at my friends: Admiral Quarto-Zar, Zaor, and huge glowering Gorm, and gave them a knowing nod, a plan had formed in my mind. If I could just get to Lord Doom, somehow get into his ship—then I might challenge him to another personal battle and hopefully kill him. Even though that seemed impossible, I knew I had to try it.

The problem was that we did not have the technology for such a physical body transfer onto Doom's warship. And another boarding party would never work now—the enemy were prepared for that. They would repel any boarders and kill them all. So the only way to do this now seemed to somehow get Doom himself to bring me over to his flagship. He had to do this willingly. Doom did have the power to do it, so my plan was a simple one. If I could contact him and challenge him, bait him, coerce him, or taunt him enough—his utter hatred of me might just cause him to bring me onto his ship in a feat of killer rage. Once I was on Doom's ship and able to confront him, who knew what I might be able to accomplish? Of course, it was most probably suicide for me, but at this point I felt it was worth a chance. I told my plan to Admiral Quarto who just shook his massive head in dire dismay. I asked him if a comm link with Doom's flagship was possible.

"It is certainly possible to send Lord Doom a message, but I can not guarantee you will get an answer."

I nodded. "So be it! Let us try! I think I will get an answer. When he hears what I have to say about him he will be stewing in his own juices so hotly he might just beam himself here to kill me personally. Then I may have a chance at him!"

I saw the warriors on the bridge grow more alert at my words and with grim smiles ready their weapons for use should Doom ever appear here.

"Yes, at least you may have a chance if he comes here," Zaor stated firmly but with obvious reluctance. Then he added, "However, he may not come here—he may take you to his own ship. If he does that, then we can not help you. Let me come with you, My Emperor."

"No Zaor, I thank you, but this is a one-man job, and it would not be possible, Doom would never take the two of us to his ship," I told him firmly. "This is my battle and my battle alone. He wants me and I shall give myself to him."

Zaor nodded sadly.

Quarto gave us a dark smile, "Still it is worth the effort, I think."

"Jon Kirk, this is madness! He will kill you immediately, whether here or on his own ship, and you will never have any opportunity to fight him one-on-one. There will be no fair fight. The man has no honor," Gorm warned with a loud growl.

"I know there is danger, but I am up to trying anything now to stop him," I replied, then I looked over to the admiral. "Give me the comm."

"If he comes here it will only be to kill you outright, or perhaps, take you to his ship to torture you at his leisure," Zaor warned me once again.

"Perhaps, but what does it matter if I die out here with you on this ship, or by the hand of Lord Doom on his own ship? At least once I am on his ship I may have a chance to get to him and slip my sword through his ribs and into his evil heart."

"I fear that will never happen, My Emperor," Admiral Quarto-Zar said in a low whisper. For a Zaran, it was their version of a death sentence.

"It is a foolhardy plan, Jon Kirk. It will most certainly lead to a trap and your death, but it is a glorious undertaking nonetheless and I wish you great luck with it." Gorm growled in excited anticipation. "I only wish I was going with you."

"I know, my friend, but stay here and help Quarto and Zaor. I am aware of the danger, but I can not think of anything better to do than to confront Doom personally. Now give me the comm."

I took a deep breath and stood tall, bold, ready to launch into a blast of harsh hard words into Doom's fetid mind. I lifted the comm and prepared to speak such words of vile hatred and insult as to make Lord Karlath Doom become so infuriated he would instantly appear on this ship to fight me—or perhaps even beam me onto his own ship. However, as it turned out I did not have to say one word, for before I ever spoke my first word, I heard a voice drilling deep within my mind, and it was Doom's own harsh words.

I have heard all that you speak and think, Jon Kirk. I am inside your ships, inside your own mind. You can not fight against me and you can not be victorious against a mind master such as I, but I will allow your wish, I will take you to my ship—now!

"No!" I heard Zaor shout.

He's gone!" the soft residue of another voice cried out in shock.

Then in the blink of an eye…

I was gone!

I found that I was gone from Admiral Quarto-Zar's command deck and was now in a large chamber on what I assumed was an alien Enemy Empire warship, and standing boldly before me with a wide hungry grin was Lord Karlath Doom himself.

I also discovered that I could not move.

"You are entirely under my control, Jon Kirk," Lord Doom spoke verbally to me, but his words also reverberated within the depths of my mind. His words commingling with my own clouded thoughts.

I acknowledged his words. Well, I had nothing to complain about. I had certainly gotten what I had wanted. I was on Lord Doom's flagship now, and now he had me just where he wanted me.

And as if reading my very thoughts—which he no doubt was doing—he told me in a voice dripping with sarcastic scorn, "And now, Jon Kirk, I have you just where I want you!"

Lord Doom's laugh dripped evil malevolence.

Meanwhile I was trapped and unable to move, and as every moment passed the black moon was speeding ever toward its deadly appointment with Ares.

CHAPTER 15

The Mind Masters

The black moon relentlessly continued on its destructive path towards Ares.

In the capital city of Tarcos upon the planet Ares, First Minister Sahn-jor convened a council of the Keven mind masters, with Lord Kneth and all the empire's master scientists under Ras-noor. It was a grim gathering and he spoke to those assembled with restrained but evident concern. Every face there was attentive and mirrored their own deep concerns, but these men and women of Ares were brave people and they would fight to find a way to win. They had no choice.

"There must be some way to destroy this black moon. Can we explode the thing using the mind powers that you all possess if they are all combined together?" Sahn-jor asked those present, trying to grasp at any slim string of hope to save their world.

They needed a plan, some course of action, as Jon Kirk had instructed him to do before the Emperor had left in their warships to fight Lord Doom's fleet. The First Minister knew these mind masters had powers far beyond anything he could ever imagine possible— but did they possess the amount of power that could stand up against their enemy and save Ares?

Lord Aron the Eldest stood up and spoke with respect, "Lord Sahn-jor, you are not aware of the actual potential of our mind powers, they are vast as I am sure you believe, but even we are limited in what we can accomplish. It is true we can meld together to increase our power and range across this planet, but we are not able to take ourselves very far into and through the void of outer space. And we are unable to explode any moon, even with Lord Kneth's valuable Sindalki aid being added to our own significant mind arts."

Sahn-jor nodded, accepting the words but not liking the limitations they implied. "But is there nothing else you can do about this?"

"Both fleets, and the black moon are still too far away for us to interfere with them," Lord Aron stated simply, shaking his head with subdued helplessness. "There does not seem to be anything we can do from here. We are too far away. We must wait. Perhaps when they get closer to Ares, then we may be able to do something."

"But by then it may be too late."

"Yes, there is that to consider," the Keven elder agreed softly, trying to keep the despair out of his voice.

There was silence for a long moment throughout the large audience chamber. Each man and woman there ensconced within their own dire thoughts that threatened to drown them with dismay. The end seemed to be closing in upon them and upon glorious Ares—meanwhile no one had heard from Jon Kirk or the fleet in many days.

It was at this darkest moment when a lovely young woman stood up tall and graceful and all attention immediately centered upon her. She had lustrous green-hued skin and dark green hair, her bright eyes were wide and full of intelligence and she pursed her bright green lips with a firm determination. She was Sirah—Empress Sirah—wife of Jon Kirk and she was now standing before the council and all the mind masters and scientists, advisors and ministers and had everyone's attention.

"Well, my friends, I for one will not accept it! Jon Kirk will not accept it! You must find a way. If a mind meld is not powerful enough, then find a way to augment it. If mind power alone will not work, perhaps the Ancient super-science of Ares can be employed in some way? Ras-noor, the ancients of Ares had all manner of super weapons and devices, did they not?"

"They did, My Lady," the old scientist admitted with a careful smile, for suddenly now something she said had sparked an idea within his venerable old brain. He wondered if what he was thinking would be possible, even as his nimble mind quickly thought through the implications. It could be extremely dangerous.

"Then let us get to it!" Empress Sirah continued in a commanding tone. She had her young son, Alun, at her side and he smiled adoringly at his mother encouraging her to continue. "Lord Kneth, I am sure there must be some dark long-forgotten Sindalki magic or power you can conjure up to help Lord Aron and the Kevens. Can you offer any thoughts?"

Lord Kneth swallowed with some difficulty at her stern tone addressed to him. He was a proud man not used to being spoken to in that manner—especially by a woman—even if she be an empress. And she was not even a Sindalki! However, he realized he had to push himself harder—if they were ever to win this war—they each had to do all they could to find a way out of Lord Doom's deadly trap.

Ras-noor looked up and posed the question carefully, "We can not explode the black moon. That seems impossible even with all our combined powers. It can not be done. However, it may not be necessary to do that. There may be another way. A simpler way. Perhaps we can find some way to deflect the black moon?"

There was sudden interest in the old scientist's words by everyone present. Hope shown in the eyes of some of the people there now.

"Go on, Ras-noor, I am interested in your words, you have our attention," Empress Sirah said with a slight smile of encouragement.

Ras-noor bowed slightly, stood a bit taller.

"Well, the black moon should be much easier to deflect than to explode, I think. It would take far less power or energy. Now at its present distance from Ares, I estimate that a four per-cent deflection angle at this time could steer it clear of Ares. I do not know how we can achieve that however. We do not possess the science, even with the super-science of the Ancients of Ares. We do not have a ray or beam powerful enough to do the work at such a distance. It seems possible in theory—I am sure it is possible to do in *theory*—but I fear that it may be impossible for us to actually achieve."

There was more silence. Deep thought's traveled among all those present.

"Well, no, I am sorry, I will not accept that! Jon Kirk, your emperor, will not accept that! There must be a way?" the empress demanded boldly in a tone of voice that did not allow any opposition.

Sahn-jor suddenly spoke up, "Noble lords, friends of Jon Kirk and our good empress, the Lady Sirah, Our Noble Lady is correct, we must find a way to explode or to deflect the black moon. There must be some way to do this. What can we do? Please offer suggestions now as time is running out. I am not a man of science or a mind master such as those noble lords who are here, so we look to you to please offer up any suggestions you may have."

"Once the moon is closer to Ares…" King Shamer of Kev began, but then he suddenly cut his words short and changed tack in his thinking. "No wait, I think not. Of course that will not work. We must do something that will allow our powers to reach the black moon *now*. Something that will expand the power we have. Lord Aron?"

Aron the Eldest nodded thoughtfully, "That is correct. I have pondered this question and there may be a way—but it is very dangerous. Lord Kneth, can you work on a new meld with my people? And you, Ras-noor, you have many amazing old machines. Do you have any that can amplify brain waves?"

Ras-noor looked up and slowly a thin smile came to his ruddy green face. "Yes, but these machines are not meant to be used as weapons, My Lord. They are merely medical devices left from the Ancients. But yes, they did have such devices that amplified various brain waves. However, I can not guarantee their results when put to use."

"Well, we have no choice now and we need to have only very specific brain waves amplified, but we need them to be very greatly amplified. I do not believe the simple small machines you have shown us will be enough. We need a massive transmitter and amplifier," Lord Aron told them.

"Well there is something—that just may be possible, My Lord. The truth is that there is not enough time to build such a massive new device as you require," Ras-noor stated carefully. "We do not have the time before that damnable moon hits Ares."

Lord Aron nodded sadly, he had thought as much.

Then Ras-noor smiled with actual excitement, "However, there may be another way. If I can link all the smaller devices we have so that they work together—into a network—into what would in effect be some kind of machine form of a mind meld—if you get my meaning—well then it may give us what we need. Then we should be able to increase the power to a truly great level. I think I can do that!"

King Shamar spoke up allowing his own excitement now to show, "That sounds like it might work. If we can amplify the power of all our mind masters—Kevens with Lord Kneth—perhaps we can achieve the level of power we need. However, there is also another way, which I hesitate to mention because of the danger. Perhaps we might enter the Dark Sphere and seek what forces may be of use to us there?"

There were looks of shock and fear by some present. This was dangerous ground to be even talking about. Others seemed to be insulted by the very thought of contacting something so sacred and mysterious—not to mention dangerous.

The Dark Sphere, was the mind land of all the people of Ares that had ever lived in all the ages of the history of the planet. It was known as the Cali-nor—the Ares equivalent of what humans called heaven—where all souls of the departed of Ares reposed, and where those souls still held some measure of power. Some sense of sentience. Each of those souls held some slight memory and mind force of who they had been in life. Individually of course their force was negligible—however together the billions upon billions of souls residing there out in the cosmos could be a force that was of incalculable power. In theory. It was known as the Sacred Ku.

"Jon Kirk and I have spoken of this once, I remember," Sahn-jor added hopefully, though he did not understand much beyond the initial concept. "He called it a universal mind."

"Yes, an interesting concept, but how do we make contact with such a field of elemental force, if in fact, it does exist? And if it exists, will it cooperate with us—or ignore us, or simply destroy us? It will be dangerous to even contact such a powerful force," Lord Kneth said showing some nervous skepticism. "The Sindalki did not often agree with the Ancients of Ares in all their ways of doing things, or with their strange beliefs. Here however is a force even the Sindalki were loath to involve themselves with."

Aron the Eldest nodded rather indulgently, "Yes, contact with the force of all those who have gone before us may be possible. At least theoretically. It may be dangerous. Almost certainly. There are billions upon billions of them, and it is a vast cosmic force that might be tapped by us, if we can do it correctly. And if it will engage with us in our request for help."

"Then let us get on it immediately," Empress Sirah ordered in all eagerness, "for time is growing short and the black moon approaches."

CHAPTER 16

Doom's Prisoner

I had achieved my plan. I had achieved what I had set out to do. Lucky me! I had caused to have myself brought aboard Lord Doom's flagship just as I had wanted to do, but now I was his helpless prisoner. I was unable to move, as I felt his thoughts probing inside my mind playing cruel tricks upon me. I had expected as much and did my best to block his thoughts and tricks. I found it almost impossible. He was too powerful a mind master. Even my own Earthly powers could not resist his dark forces.

"You can never win against me, Jon Kirk," Doom's voice shouted into my mind, obscuring my very thoughts. "I have a hundred times your power, and my master, the Kin-Ty-Roo, has a hundred times my own power! So you see, we are unbeatable!"

"Nothing and no one is unbeatable, Doom," I replied boldly, fiercely proud, though his control over me only allowed me verbal and mental communication, but no other physical movement at all. "Anything or anyone, can be killed. Even you!"

"Hah!" he snarled. "I may be killed but I can never truly die! No one knows that better than you, Jon Kirk!"

"You can die and will die! Especially you!" I shouted, the images in my mind reminding him of our past fight where I had defeated him and caused his death—one time already. His death had not taken hold however.

Doom just laughed, showing typical Sindalki arrogance, "Hah, oh yes that may be true, for you did once kill me a short time ago, Jon Kirk. Yes, you actually killed me! You bested me in a sword fight and plunged your blade into my heart. Well, how did that work out? I died and then I brought myself back to life. And now I am here alive and with all my powers greater than ever—and in full control of you!

You are my prisoner and helpless. No, Jon Kirk, you cannot win. You can never win!"

"I shall defeat you again, and this time it will be forever!" I barked back in utter determination.

"Those are just bold words spoken by a desperate man. However, I shall not kill you just yet, for I see within you there is this love you have for your mate, your child, and the world of Ares. That interests me. Love? What is it? I feel no such emotion. And yet it runs so vastly deep within you—this thing you call love—you have a heart that even befriends a Winged-man of Zar of all the vile beasts! It seems that it is that very same Quarto-Zar who betrayed me—I see he has been made the admiral now on your fleet opposing my own—and yet this Winged-man is a creature you have true admiration, respect, and even friendship for? It is amazing! Most disgusting actually! I can not understand this. I can see no reason for it. None of it makes any sense to me."

"That is because I am a human being and we have feelings and respect life. You are a monster—a creature! I am from Earth, you remember Earth? You destroyed it! And you shall pay heavily for that, I promise you!" I cried my words in rage for they were burning like fire within my empty painful heart—and they were all I could use to fight against him now, for I could not move my body at all, and I was under his complete control physically.

Lord Doom just laughed disdainfully once again, allowing full vent to that insulting smirk upon his face, and his superior type laugh I had grown to hate. He was obviously enjoying himself. "Ah, yes, Earth, a nothing backwater world better dead and gone. It pained you greatly, did it not, to see it so utterly destroyed? So many lived there who are dead now. Did you know any of them?"

"Yes, you know it pained me greatly and I did know some of them."

"Of course, Jon Kirk, and that is precisely why I did it when I did. I can see the horror of it all even now writhing like the coils of an oily serpent within your mind. The great pain it has caused you is still there—I find it incredible—but it is so good to see such deep suffering within you. I like to see it. It seems that it never leaves you, does it not? So sad really—for you—though it brings me much happiness," Doom said with a dismissive malevolent grin. He was enjoying my suffering. He was a most cunning and devious demon.

"I promise you that you will pay for that, and everything you have done!"

"No, I think not, Jon Kirk. In fact, with the power of the Kin-Ty-Roo behind me, I shall soon become master of all this part of Known Space—the area you so simplistically call the Known Universe. Then maybe I shall proclaim myself Emperor of this so-called Known Universe—a title by the way that I believe you very much misappropriated. I shall set that right soon as well."

"The emperorship was thrust upon me by the people I serve!"

"How quaint. These 'people' as you call them, a hodge-podge of alien races, mutants and lower beast things, beings who only exist to serve. Gorns, Kortas, Zaran Winged-men! Blah! They are nothing. Well, they shall all serve me soon once again, and the Kin-Ty-Roo. Or they shall all die."

I looked hard at Lord Doom then.

"Tell me something—if you even know anything about it. What exactly is this Kin-Ty-Roo?" I asked Doom, my tone daring him to answer. He seemed momentarily surprised by the question, a sharp change of tack for me that he may not have anticipated.

He looked at me closely and did not reply to me right away.

I pressed him, "I see. So even you are afraid to speak of him?"

"Him? Hah, how little you know, how little you realize. So I shall tell you now. The Kin-Ty-Roo is not male, in fact it has no gender as such—it is an 'it'—a thing—a primal force that exists to devour. To feed. I do not know why, but it has an insatiable appetite to devour—and to absorb beings of all kinds within itself. Entire races, worlds even. It is not something of this galaxy, not of the Known Universe around us, but something that has entered here from Outside. Far Outside. Where this Outside is located, I have no idea. Even I, a great Sindalki lord, do not possess that kind of far-seeing knowledge. However, the Kin-Ty-Roo seems to have ultimate power, some would certainly consider it to be a god. It does so itself, I am sure. It is an all-powerful, all-consuming entity with no purpose that I can see other than to continue what it has been doing since the beginning of time. Consuming all matter and energy that it encounters."

I looked at Lord Doom carefully, his words shocked me. I was sure he was being truthful. I felt a terrible chill tremble throughout my body at what I had just heard. I wondered if such a thing could even be possible—then I knew that in this universe we inhabit—it certainly could be possible.

"You are fearful of it."

Lord Doom bristled with anger at the affront to him by my pointed question, then slowly he admitted, "Yes, even I, a great Sindalki lord—the last of the great Sindalki race—do fear the Kin-Ty-Roo. Not to do so would be foolish and a vast mistake."

"And now what of me?"

"You, my dear Jon Kirk, have caused me considerable trouble, and I seek to pay you back in kind, but not just yet," Doom told me savoring the moment. "No, you shall not be killed immediately as you thought you would be. You will live, at least long enough to see your little crimson world of Ares crushed and destroyed and all the people you know upon it burned into fiery ash as they die a horrible death. And you will know that it was I, Lord Karlath Doom, who made all this come to pass. Earth and Ares, will both soon be memories in the minds of beings who no longer exist, and then I shall alleviate your suffering by feeding you to the Kin-Ty-Roo myself. That shall be your fate, Jon Kirk. The entity will feed upon you. What do you have to say to that?"

"I say you will never win. I say you will never destroy Ares. I say your fleet is in trouble and I promise you that some day I shall kill you for real Doom, and it will be the certain death of eternity for you!"

"And yet you are my helpless prisoner."

"Yes, I am your prisoner. For now."

"Hah, so it is all bold talk and flowery words but they shall not bring you victory this time, Jon Kirk."

"I know that, Doom, but you see, there is much more to me than bold talk and flowery words."

"We shall see."

"Yes, we shall see."

"Well, as pleasurable as this conversation has been for me, I have other more serious matters to attend to. So now, I must turn my attentions to the fleet and the battle that will cause the destruction of all your ships and crews," Doom stated with a sly smile of anticipatory glee. He was up to something devious. "In the mean time I place you into the capable hands of three of my most loyal surrogates. They are truly worthy captors and enjoy inflicting pain and suffering. They will enjoy holding you their prisoner. I believe you may even known them. They are also from the planet Ares."

I looked askance, not knowing what to expect from this madman, but sure that it would be terrible. I had no idea just how terrible it would be. I remained frozen in position as a helpless prisoner when I was astounded to see three men I had never thought to ever see again this side of Hell enter the room.

They were Crooch, Vakon and Tob.

"Lord Doom!" they each chanted and saluted their master, and now I saw all my greatest enemies together in one room and me help- less to do anything about them. It was sheer torture to see them there and alive—but my real torture had not yet begun. They looked at me and smiled grim looks of impending promises of vicious terror.

"My fine fellows, entertain our visitor here until I return," Doom ordered, and then he was gone. As soon as he was gone I instantly collapsed to the floor as his mind control over me had been immedi- ately terminated.

However, that quick release did not offer me any escape. I was still unable to move after being held in stasis for so long a time, my muscles were numb and weak, too weak to even stand up right away. Even as the fire in my body—in my very heart and soul at the sight of these three traitors and vile creatures shone through my eyes with burning anger. I shouted in rage, cursing each one of them.

"Ah, yes, Jon Kirk, we see you are happy to see us, and it is good to see you again, as well," Crooch replied to my insults in that oily voice of his, as he, with Vakon and Tob by his side, approached me right away. They quickly bound me with chains and shackles so I could not move. I was once again a helpless prisoner. "We will be your companions until Ares is no more. And then after we have had our fun—you shall also be no more!"

The deadly trio laughed mocking me in every way.

Tob came over to me, his hot putrid breath in my face as he said, "Jon Kirk, do you know that the Lady Sirah has been promised to me by Lord Doom? He is a most generous master. I shall have my way with her in many interesting ways!"

"You shall never have her!" I cried out at him in red murderous rage.

Tob just laughed, mocking me as he did so. Tob, formerly a king of the warrior caste—that same caste of fighters now led by Zaor—was as deadly a traitor and enemy as I had ever met on Ares. Only the oily slug Crooch bested him in sheer treachery.

My eyes spewed stark hatred at the trio but my words were silent for there was nothing else I could say or do about this situation unless I could become free—and that did not appear to be in the cards at all. I was most securely bound in shackles and chains and at the mercy of this traitorous trio.

CHAPTER 17

The Black Moon Rises

On Ares the mood was grim, but they had not given up. Aron the Eldest formed a ring with all the Keven mind masters, along with Lord Kneth, while Ras-noor had brought in a most unusual device or machine to the gathering. Sahn-jor and Empress Sirah looked on with interest and deep concern at what was about to take place. They did not allow themselves the luxury of hope yet, but they were most curious.

"The black moon grows closer, but it is still far enough away from Ares to be diverted and so not harm our world, if we act immediately," Ras-noor stated confidently. "If what we plan to do now works. That is the big question. This controlling device is connected to a hundred like it in other areas of the palace, and it should be able to augment the Keven brain waves a hundred fold—perhaps even a thousand fold or more."

"Good," Lord Aron replied hopefully, "then let us get started. We have much work to do and little time to do it. Let us form a ring, attune our minds, and create the meld."

The Keven mind masters, with Lord Kneth joining them now, sat upon the floor in a large circle. They did not touch each other, no holding hands or any physical contact was permitted or necessary—but they were all most certainly in close mental contact. Their minds were all linked with each other, and with Aron the Eldest who was now their controller and focused their thoughts and power in one particular direction.

"Now, brethren, listen closely. We are going to join together as one being, I will be your guide, your Controller, Lord Kneth attend me please. We will transport our minds far off into the cosmos all around us and into the beyond. Are you ready?"

There was no verbal or even mind answer to the question but all there were ready.

"Then let us begin," Lord Aron stated with firm resolve. "What we do now will decide the future of Ares and all the worlds that make up the Known Universe."

Then Lord Aron began to deeply concentrate and as he did so he started to hum in a very low tone to himself, which was soon joined by all the members of the circle. It was amazing to see and hear some four dozen Keven mind masters grow rigid in rapt concentration and then hum along with him. The tone was low but distinct—much like the buzzing of earthly bees Jon Kirk would have described it, had he been present—but of course, he was not. Lord Kncth had contributed what he could of his deep knowledge of secret Sindalki magic to enable the meld to meet a new level of height that was necessary for the work ahead.

The mind meld grew in power and resonance. Lord Aron was amazed that he was able to focus so much mental energy at a single pinpoint source and then push it outward, through the atmosphere of Ares, and far into the vast airless reaches of outer space. Still the mind meld held firmly and the pattern of mental force moved their vision far outward from Ares, outward towards its destination of the black moon.

"We are making progress," Aron's mind told all in the meld with evident surprise at the success they had achieved so far, and then into Ras-noor's mind he sent the command, "You may turn on your machine, scientist."

Ras-noor was amazed at what he was witnessing, little realizing the immense power that was present there because it seemed so silent and still. He turned on his machine. There was little noise. There was no great rush of energy, no loud sound as from large and great machines—other than the low humming buzz of the mind masters. There was no cataclysm or turmoil. There was only the silent manifestation of some presence that he could not explain. It was most strange. He was a scientist, not one who held any great knowledge of the mental arts or mind powers as these mysterious Kevens did, or as Lord Kneth did, but he knew something special and remarkable was occurring on this day here and now among them.

Ras-noor quickly checked his machine once more, then turned the control to the highest setting. He did not quite understand this mysterious brain wave machine, it was one of those left behind millennia ago by the venerated Ancients of Ares. It did not seem to do much of anything at first. He had connected it to a hundred similar devices, but this one was the master, the controller. The controller of all his similar machines, and somehow Lord Aron was able to connect to it and control it as well. The machine gave off very little sound, only a low hum, almost in tune with the humming sound Lord Aron and the mind masters were making now while in their mind meld trance. The two sounds seemed to coalesce. They co-joined, became one, and then met at exactly the same pitch.

It was then when Ras-noor noticed a stunning shock come upon each member of the meld ring, as if they had been hit with a bolt of electricity—though he knew it was not any power as mundane as mere electricity. The machine had somehow augmented the brain waves of the Kevens, augmented them massively, apparently just enough to push their powers to the brink of where they needed to be. Ras-noor wondered if it would be enough and what dangers such power posed to the mind masters themselves. He feared he smelt the odor of burning flesh, worried over frayed brains damaged by powerful forces of energy that perhaps should never be invoked by men.

"Take it farther out now, tighten the beam brothers, and let us push ourselves harder, deeper into the void of darkest space," Lord Aron cried out in a powerful tone verbally and mentally. His voice was tinged with nervous fear and excitement.

Ras-noor wondered what the old man saw, what could it be that was putting such fear—even terror—into such a powerful mind master?

Aron the Eldest suddenly began to shake with tremors, though he seemed to ignore them. "We must push deeper still, the black moon is near, I can feel it. I can almost touch it. I can see it now! Can you not see it as well, brothers?"

There was the continual low hum and then a soft murmur of reply.

"We are almost there," Lord Aron said in a shaky tone that implied fear and hope.

Ras-noor saw that one of the Keven mind masters, Larl, now spoke up in dire warning, "It is the Kin-Ty-Roo! It is seeking us! Lord Aron, it is searching the void of deep space to contact us and control us. We must complete our mission now before it is too late. Before it can initiate contact with us. If the Kin-Ty-Roo makes contact with our meld…"

"Yes, I am aware of the danger. It could control us all," Lord Aron warned, fully understanding the immediate danger to them all now by having their minds becoming so attuned to the mind of the alien entity enemy.

There was stunned quiet and growing fear that hung like a physical thing within that room now. The danger of contact with the alien entity could be a disaster.

The Keven mind master continued. "I am aware of the danger but it will not happen. Give me the best you have left within you, brothers. Give me all the power you can give and we will complete this mission immediately and save Ares. I see the black moon hurling out towards Ares now. I see it as plainly as if it were here already. I can now touch it with my mind. It is vast, a devastating missile of enormous mass, but it can be reached and diverted. And while we may not have the power to explode it, we do have the power to deflect it to another course that will take it away from Ares."

There was silence for a moment as each member of the ring forced themselves to add every last erg of power and force they had within them to the meld. They were exhausted and trembling.

Ras-noor noticed the sweat dripping from the faces of many of the men in that meld. King Shamar jumped up to help one of the weaker and more feeble of the group when he apparently fainted.

"It is of no consequence," Lord Kneth observed firmly. "I am fully able to compensate for the loss of Torok in the meld. It will just cost me more energy than I had thought I would need to expend. I will just dig deeper within myself, as we all have done. I give all my energy willingly now. Every last bit of it!"

"We are almost there, brothers," Lord Aron spoke up in earnest, excitement tingeing his rasping words. "The black moon has a force field or shield of some type around it, to protect it from being exploded. That is no problem for us. We have no desire to explode it. We are going to divert it, and even now, the black moon has been tilted five per-cent, which is more than necessary to ensure that it changes its course and will pass harmlessly by Ares. It is done! We have done it! Ares is saved, my brothers! The black moon shall not harm us—now let us immediately break this meld and bring our minds back to Ares before the entity can make contact with us out in the far void of space."

The mind meld was immediately broken. None too soon. Ras-noor quickly turned off his machine. Aron the Eldest tried to stand up on his feet but he was dizzy, an attendant helped him. Lord Kneth collapsed, but it was just due to utter exhaustion, for each of the mind masters felt the same great drain of energy.

"We have been successful!" Lord Aron spoke up greatly tired but with a new boldness to the members of his mind meld group, and the others who were in attendance in that vast chamber who had witnessed the mind meld.

Empress Sirah, and First Minister Sahn-jor, who had looked on from their seats in the front of the room, but who had not been involved in the actual event, let out a deep sigh of relief. It was over. By all aspects they had been successful.

"It is done!" Lord Kneth stated firmly, even victoriously.

"Ares is secure," Lord Aron added and Ras-noor nodded in happy agreement. They had, in fact, done it.

"Thank you, My Lords! Then we have diverted the black moon! Ares is saved!" Empress Sirah shouted her words in joyous victory, even as her wounded heart wondered where Jon Kirk was now, and how he was doing on his own so very dangerous mission. Ares was safe, but what of her husband? Was Jon Kirk even alive? She tried not to think those grim thoughts now. She held back her tears and proclaimed victory loudly now for the benefit of her people. They deserved it. "Let us all rejoice! Ares is saved!"

Sahn-jor allowed a wry smile, and in a low voice added to the empress at his side, "At least for now, My Lady. At least for now."

CHAPTER 18

The Great Betrayer

I was still held a helpless prisoner on Lord Doom's massive space battleship, which was just one ship within his vast fleet, and merely one war vessel of his master, the alien entity known as the Kin-Ty-Roo. I was in chains and heavy shackles. I was being held under close supervision by three armed men. These were three men of Ares who had become my greatest enemies and were despised traitors. Monsters all!

Crooch, Vakon and Tob, had suddenly resurfaced into my life at the worst possible moment and now they held me captive in chains under their master Lord Doom—who was no doubt on the bridge of this very flagship now directing his fleet in the destruction of my own fleet led by Admiral Quarto-Zar.

How had things become so complicated?

I tried my best to escape, of course, to slip the chains on my wrists—or break them—somehow to get free of the heavy metal shackles that bound my legs and feet, but it was impossible. It was almost as if these restraint devices had been especially created to hold me locked in captivity. To keep me held as a helpless prisoner. I certainly was a prisoner now. I found myself at the mercy of Crooch, Vakon and Tob, and I knew that I could not expect any quarter or mercy from the likes of them.

Tob was the worst. He kept on taunting me with the news that he would soon sample the supple flesh of my beloved Sirah, for Doom had promised her to him. I knew the former king of the warrior caste of Ares had long desired my Lady Sirah, and he had abducted her on at least two occasions in the past—but I had always been there in time and was able to crush his vile plans and save her. Now I was not so sure.

Meanwhile, miserable little Vakon proved to be a sadistic monster who taunted me in other ways, with tiny physical tortures, inflicting pain upon my body in various places using a thin sharp blade. It was like an ice-pick and he cut away at me with it in small teasing slashes and light punctures, and he just laughed at my pain as he did so. However, he seemed careful not to cause me any serious injury, at least not yet, for that was not his goal at the moment, but the pain he inflicted upon me was quite enough, causing me constant annoying hurtful agony that seemed to give him much pleasure. The man was the worse kind of sadistic monster, but I was able to put up with his simple tortures without any sound or comment. That seemed to annoy him. The more silent I was, the more anxious and angry he became, for I was not reacting at all to his torture as he had expected. Even though I was held fast and unable to do anything to free myself, I would never give Vakon the satisfaction that his actions were even noticed by me. I ignored it all, placing my mind and thoughts somewhere else more pleasant. Dreaming of sweet lovely Sirah, and my young son, Alun. Would I ever see them again? I did my best to force those negative thoughts from my mind, to close off the fear about never seeing them again, but the thoughts were there always at the edge of my mind nagging at me nevertheless, causing me more true pain than Vakon ever could.

However, it was Crooch, the most deadly and devious of the trio that caused me the most concern. He was a far more treacherous and enigmatic enemy. While he made verbal threats to me, and even spoke of the coming destruction of the entire planet of Ares when his two companions were around, he did not inflict any physical pain or torture upon me. He did seem to look at me closely, rather intently, seeming to see me as if he had done so for the first time. It was most strange. Something was definitely up with him that I could not figure out. Had he gone mad? I wondered. That possibility did get me nervous and I feared what he might be up to. For he was the most devious and deadly of the trio. I feared what he might be planning—for I was sure he was up to something to make my captivity even more miserable than it already was.

Once his companions left me, Crooch came in close and once more looked deeply into my eyes. I wondered what he was looking for, what he saw there inside me. Fear? I thought at first that was it, that he might be under the mind control of Lord Doom—or worse yet, the entity called the Kin-Ty-Roo—but soon enough I realized that it did not seem to be so at all. It was most strange to me.

"Crooch?" I asked, looking back at him firmly in the eyes, his eyes staring blankly into my own. It was weird. I wondered what was up with him now. Was he ill? Had he gone mad?

"Jon Kirk," he whispered softly, then repeated, "Yes, you are Jon Kirk."

"That's my name," I replied mockingly.

"Yes it is," he said softly, but seriously.

"What is it you want?" I asked, for I was sure this was the reason for his strange and inexplicable behavior—he wanted something from me—though what I had to give at this point seemed meaningless. So what did this treacherous villain want?

"I am in need of… I want to ask you something…" he stammered with evident difficulty, as if he were the one in chains and not I. It was a most strange arrangement and I grew very curious about what was in his mind. We were alone now, and it was quiet.

"What is it?"

"Tell me about this—the Kin-Ty-Roo."

I looked back at him curiously, rather surprised by this question, but he was apparently deadly serious. By now Tob had wandered off to the other end of the room, and Vakon had grown weary of torturing me as I had never uttered a sound to his petty stabbings and slashes, so Vakon had become bored and now sat at a far table eating and drinking with Tob.

Crooch and I were alone for the first time now.

"You want something? What is it you want of me?" I asked the great villain, for I had decided to play his game and see where it led. I knew very little about the alien entity, but Doom had told me some interesting information about it.

"Tell me, Jon Kirk, what I want to know most, is this: Do you think it will it ever stop?" Crooch asked me in all seriousness. It was the most enigmatic question I ever would have thought possible by one such as he.

"Will it ever stop? What do you mean? Stop feeding? Devouring? No, I do not think it will ever stop any of this activity from what I have been told," I answered simply, truthfully, as far as I knew.

"Does it truly absorb living creatures for food?"

"Yes it absorbs them as far as I have been told—but I know not if for food in the conventional way we think of it."

He nodded nervously, "Then will it absorb us all?"

"Yes, eventually," I replied looking him dead-on in the eyes.

I saw him shiver then, "I hear tell it can even absorb entire planets. Even Ares?"

"Yes, that is what I have been told, unless it is stopped."

"Then that is the key question upon which everything must settle. Are you the right man? Can you stop it?" Crooch asked me seriously.

"What? What do you mean?" I looked at him in shock and surprise, but he was most serious.

"Can you stop it, Jon Kirk?" he repeated his question.

"I do not know. I will do my damnedest to try, if ever given the opportunity, but I am otherwise occupied at the moment, as you can see." I told him, rattling my chains to lend emphasis to my words that I was but a helpless prisoner now.

"I believe you, Jon Kirk, for I know you are an honorable man," Crooch told me softly, giving me a most enigmatic but compelling look that I could not describe. It was almost surreal. Then he added most truthfully, "I know you are not a liar. You are a man of great honor and integrity—you value your honor and integrity. I on the other hand am one who possesses neither."

"As I can readily attest to," I taunted him back now. I could not resist it.

Crooch allowed one of his oily smiles to show through, and for a brief moment I feared the old Crooch was back and that he would do me ill, but then his face grew taut and his eyes bored into my own, "Yes, you are correct, but there is something that even a man like you should know about a man like me, Jon Kirk."

"And what might that be, Crooch?" I said allowing my skepticism to show.

"That being a bad person, while often ignoble and even despicable, is not always necessarily the same thing as being—evil. There is a vast chasm between bad and evil. I have no wish to bridge that gap. I have no wish to be absorbed by that thing, and I have no wish to serve anything like that alien entity. I have seen what it has done to a powerful Sindalki like Lord Doom. I have seen how service to this Kin-Ty-Roo, this monster with no name, has twisted the mind and soul of all who serve it, how it has taken over even Lord Doom's heart and life, and made of it a dark black thing like that moon that is now hurtling towards Ares. I seek another way. A better way. Can you help me, Jon Kirk?"

"I help you? You forget, I am the prisoner here," I reminded him, wondering just what he was up to.

"Yes, but still I am asking for your help," Crooch insisted in all seriousness.

To say that I was astounded by his words would have been a vast understatement. Even more unnerving was that his words even seemed to ring with the genuine tone of truth. Quite amazing for a fellow like Crooch. However, I took care to remind myself that this man was a most devious and cunning monster himself. And a supreme liar. Treacherous. Treachery was his byword. Nevertheless, I wondered what was behind his words? What had he seen? What was it that so bothered him? And then, I think, I figured it out.

"Fear has you in its clutches. I can see that now. Something you have seen here has scared you like you have never been scared in your life," I told Crooch firmly. It was not a question but a statement of fact.

He was silent for a long moment, but I could see his hands shaking. His face was twitching nervously. That caught my attention.

Finally he nodded grimly, "Yes, you have no idea what I have seen, you have no idea. Now will you help me, Jon Kirk?"

"Well, I will if I am able, but only if you can help me, Crooch," I responded boldly, and this remark proved to be the beginning of an alliance I had never ever thought possible.

Crooch allowed a cunning smile to cross his face, as he took out a small device from the folds of his robe and pressed the red button upon it. Immediately my chains and shackles automatically unlocked and dropped to the floor. All encumbrances holding me back were now unleashed.

I was unbound and free!

I was amazed!

Crooch then further amazed me when he quickly placed a short sword into my hand, along with returning to me my trusty old Colt .45 auto into my other hand. I was astonished he even had my weapons so accessible, obviously he had put some thought into this action beforehand. "Here, you will have need of these. Make good use of them. Stop Lord Doom. I shall remain here and entertain my companions, then I will join you later. Good hunting, Jon Kirk. Be victorious. I believe in you."

For a moment I stood there in total amazement by what had just happened and what I had heard from the mouth of the most treacherous man I have ever met in my life. Was this some new twisted form of torture? I had no way of knowing. However, I would not waste any time thinking about it. I quickly moved to make the most of the opportunity that had been given to me. I knew what I must do. I ran off to find Lord Doom.

I saw Crooch run off as well, withdrawing a ray pistol from his robes. I got a glimpse of him as he began to aim his death ray weapon to attack Tob and Vakon. Crooch proved not to be a very good shot so that soon the three were engaged in fighting a vicious battle among each other with death ray weapons.

I quickly left them and escaped the room.

Outside the room and free now, I found myself alone in a long and wide hallway. I was determined to find my way through the ship to get to the bridge where I would confront Lord Doom. Then I would take his life.

However, as I continued down the outer hall, and ran deeper into that long wide hallway of the massive battleship, I suddenly came upon Lord Doom walking briskly towards me from the other end of the long hallway. His footsteps were bold and purposeful.

"Jon Kirk!" Doom shouted at me in anger.

"Doom!" I barked back, moving forward, ready to attack him.

"So it is true! I had an advance premonition you had somehow become free, Jon Kirk, even though I could not believe it possible," Doom told me almost casually now, having tamped down his rage. "So tell me, who was it? Tob? No, I promised him your wife as his plaything. Did you know that? Then it must be that wicked little sadist, Vakon, I assume? He is certainly contemptible but sometimes he can be most entertaining. He is always looking for more blood to be spilled. Yet now I wonder?"

"It was Crooch," I replied to him sharply.

"Ah, yes, goodly Crooch, of course, he is the smartest and most devious of the three. Yet it is of little consequence to me now. I assume they are now busy killing each other."

"I certainly hope so."

"So now it seems it is down to you and I once again. It must be destiny that we meet like this here alone, is it not?"

I nodded, drawing and pointing my Colt .45 auto directly at Lord Doom, then without further delay, I immediately began firing. My aim was good as ever. My slugs hit the target every time, going straight and true into his chest and head but he was obviously protected by some kind of personal shielding or force field. He was also wearing a black helm and black body armor that may have held his force field shielding. I knew it was too good to be true. He just laughed at my paltry attack upon him. The slugs from my gun just deflected off him and soon my .45 auto was empty. I knew I would have to go to other means now. I put my .45 back into the holster on my belt and withdrew my short sword, quickly planning on how best to advance against him.

Lord Karlath Doom smiled with evil delight at the sight of my sword out and ready to do battle with him. I had bested him with just such a sword a short time ago once before. Now I was ready again to confront him with another sword and he saw me and said, "I shall not place you in stasis again, Jon Kirk. No, not this time. You may be much too dangerous, but I think we shall fight this battle one-on-one. Now we shall have that re-match we have both wanted for so long—even as your fleet is being taken down and your ships will soon all be destroyed. We shall fight it out one against the other, even as the black moon hurls towards Ares on its mission of destruction. You and I will decide our fate here and now once and for all. I believe that it is our destiny, that we fight this one last great battle."

"Then make the most of it, you son of a bitch!" I growled, gripping my sword tightly, formulating my plan of attack as I moved in closer upon him.

"Indeed I shall. We fought once, a personal battle with swords, and we shall do so again now to the end," Doom said with evident delight.

In my hand was a good Ares short sword, very similar to the one I had used to kill Doom only scant weeks before. I tested the heft and sharpness of the blade. It would do. It was well-balanced and razor sharp, a good killing weapon. I silently thanked Crooch for this precious gift. Crooch, who had made all this possible. He had come to my aid at the very moment that I needed help. I hardly knew what to think of him now.

"I am ready, let's get to it!" I barked simply, for as a fighting man, all I ever want is a good weapon and a chance to use it to defeat my enemy, and it appeared that here and now I had all that I needed to be successful.

Doom withdrew his own long sword, an enormous two-handed blade of immense destructive power. If he ever cut me with that blade it would be all over for me. I had to stay away from that powerful sharp edge and the striking power of that blade.

I tested my own sword's balance with a few quick strokes and flourishes. I was comfortable with such a blade. I was ready.

"This shall be a fair fight. Personal combat to the death on the Physical Plane only—it shall go on until your death—for even should you win this fight, know that I shall use my powers to regenerate. Then we shall be at it again until you are eventually defeated. It shall be quick and I shall not be merciful. I have no need of any superscience or my mind master powers to dull your attack or defeat you, Jon Kirk. This is, after all, what you always wanted. I saw it in your mind, like I can see everything. You only wanted one chance to get at me. One-on-one without any interferences. So be it! So here we are. Take your chance now!"

CHAPTER 19

Battle is Joined

"I will take it now!" I shouted and quickly rushed upon him with a fierce attack of forward lunges and hard strikes that seemed to quite surprise him with the ardor of my attack.

Lord Doom moved back a bit stunned by the ferocity of my blade, but careful, even smiling. It was unnerving to see him recover so soon. Then he came at me hurling that huge two-handed broadsword like it was a toy. I deftly kept away from his massive blade as I worked to get around his guard to hit him back with deadly cuts and thrusts—none of which had yet connected. I moved quickly, my Earthly muscles standing me in good stead, and his large weapon just missed me by inches. Nevertheless, he came too close to me for comfort with his sharp blade. I often escaped that deadly edge just in time.

I continued to move around him quickly, never standing for a moment in one spot. My body moved all around the area. My sword was weaving in and out of Lord Doom's guard in an effort to strike him with a flanking blow. He was fast, even using such a large and unwieldy blade, but I was faster. I had to be. My Earthly muscles allowed me rare vast strength and endurance, and this at first surprised Doom—even though we had fought previously and he should have remembered my Earthly speed and agility. I thanked my lucky star that he had apparently forgotten about that superior Earthly energy and agility. And yet, he was fast and agile also, but somewhat hampered by his massive heavy two-handed blade which seemed to hold him back just a bit. It must have weighed a ton, but its weight seemed not to be a major problem for him, though I can tell you it did cut down his movement and agility—and it made me most cautious ever to make sure that it never got anywhere near me.

Indeed, my main aim at that point was to do all I could to get in a good stabbing blow, even as I stayed away from Doom's deadly blade, for if it ever connected with me, I was a goner. I moved and rolled away, then rolled back and struck him as hard as I was able. I connected, slashing and tearing his armor, but not into his flesh.

We continued to clash blades hard and deadly, and my hand and arm shook with the clang and vibration from smacking against his heavy blade. I quickly parried his slashes, stepped back from his own great downward slashes in an attempt to rip open my chest, and then replied with a renewed thrust at his head.

I missed.

I moved back and looked around me quickly to get my bearings. Taking stock of the situation. The huge hallway was still empty and we were still alone as I moved forward again and towards him to begin another attack. He let me come at him, smiling, waiting. I grew nervous about the way the battle was progressing. It was not going the way I hoped that it would. I was quickly beginning to realize that I was in serious trouble.

Nevertheless I fought on, while in the back of my mind I grew suspicious, for I was sure now that Doom knew my innermost thoughts. He was apparently reading my mind somehow so he had an idea of what action I would take next, what I thought, how I would come at him. At least it seemed to be so, for he seemed always to be ready for me. Waiting. Almost anticipating my every move.

Doom's face showed me that supercilious smirk visible through the open front of his black helm, it was the sure arrogance of the overly prideful Sindalki lord. I knew I had to do something to impede him. I tried to confuse him, masking my thoughts, changing my plan of attack at the last moment. I used the powers of my Earthly human mind to mask my thoughts as much as possible. I filled it with hate and anger directed towards him. I used opposite logic. It seemed to help, Earthly and Ares minds are not exactly alike, so that there are some differences. However, I soon realized that even this plan was merely delaying the inevitable and that I was not winning the fight. In fact Doom seemed to be just playing with me, and that this had probably been his plan from the very beginning. He was apparently enjoying it. I knew I was in a tough spot.

"Ah, so I see you have figured it out, Jon Kirk. Very good. In truth, it will almost be a shame to kill someone with as much potential as you. But really, Emperor of the Known Universe? There is only one being that can lay claim to such a title and that is myself— or the Great Master I serve—meanwhile your feelings of honor and fairness that I see within you truly sicken me. You are weak and these feelings make you weak. I think it is time we end this. Farewell, Jon Kirk. You were never meant for this world."

"We'll see about that!" I growled back in defiant anger.

Suddenly Lord Doom came at me with a renewed flurry of hard, pummeling strikes and vicious slashes that pushed me back into a fearful and dire defense. It was a stress inducing attack and had me moving back to get out of his range. That huge double-handed sword of his struck around me slamming into the metal of the deck and wall of his ship, sometimes hitting my blade and when it did, it slammed it hard, vibrating my hand with a pain that ran upwards along my arm to my shoulder—even as I did everything I could to make sure that his blade never blooded me. So far it had not. I knew that if it ever did, it would be the end of me. I did not have much time. My lean short sword was barely able to impede his attack and put up a worthy defense against his fierce weapon, and I knew that soon it would be all over for me if I did not change this situation right away.

I needed to get in close to my enemy where my short sword could do the most damage. I needed to clench with him and then thrust my sword quickly and deeply into his vitals. And even as I thought these thoughts, making my plan, I knew that he was reading those thoughts and smiling with grim satisfaction. He seemed to be reading me like a book. I was in deep trouble for he knew my every thought—but I decided to use that against him now. I made a plan back in the recesses of my mind that was the exact opposite of what I would do, and it was a plan that counted on the very fact that he was reading my mind.

Doom came at me again, harder this time, oozing confidence now. He was enjoying himself, anticipating a sweet bloody victory. This was a far different battle than the one we had engaged in days ago back on Ares. There Lord Aron and the Kevens had aided me in blocking my enemy from reading my thoughts. Then I had bested Doom in a fair battle. This was not like that at all. This time, I did not have anyone's help to keep the various mind forces on a level basis, so while I was fairly sure of the outcome, I knew that it did not bode well for me this time.

Well, we would see about that!

I allowed Doom inside my mind to track my thoughts, I could not prevent him from doing so anyway, so I made them as plain as possible. Nothing complicated. I kept it simple; stark emotions of hate and fear collided with guilt and rage. Anger and terror. He sneered at me, then laughed. He was surely tasting victory. I allowed him to do so.

I moved back from him, looking fearful, showing terror now, which egged him on as if it were some drug he could not resist. He could taste my fear and defeat. I allowed that fear to grow, and to show. It was not all fake fear, let me tell you, but I allowed it to run rampant in my mind. Most of it was genuine, for I feared I might never see my beloved Sirah again, or little Alun, or Ares itself. I could still lose this battle.

Doom came onwards, more reckless now, fearless. He did not care about my defenses, he did not care about my attack, he would end this battle soon. He saw me as easy pickings and I allowed him to see that outcome. Finally I had afforded him enough amusement and now he was ready to strike and end it all. He was in full red mist battle mode now—the kill zone. I gave him a little more room, then went down low, rolled forward under his blade, just missing a massive downward stroke that could have cut me in half had it connected, and then I barreled into his legs. Doom collapsed on top of me.

He was down now!

I quickly reversed our positions and lifted my short blade, knocking Doom's massive sword out of his hands. It flew across the hallway. Then I took my blade and quickly plunged it into the sweet spot upon his body that I knew would end it. The death blow.

I drove my sword point directly into the eye slit of Lord Doom's helmet, and it found no shielding or force field there, but only soft tissue that gave way to my blade. I plunged my blade down deep, down into his head, into his brain, into his very mind and then I twisted the blade to do the most damage possible.

I barked at him in furious rage, "When you were inside my mind learning my secrets, know that I was in contact with your mind also learning some of your own secrets. Your mind is your most potent weapon and your most delicate and vulnerable area. Goodbye, Lord Doom, die now and may you rot in Hell!"

I pushed in my blade deeper and twisted it yet again. His body shuddered and then lay still.

He was dead!

But was he really, totally, *truly* dead?

That was the real question!

How could I be sure?

The life went out of him rather quickly. He was dead now, for certain I thought—or I hoped. But was he dead *for good*? I looked down upon the dead corpse of Lord Karlath Doom, it did not move, but that in and of itself did not mean anything just yet. I took nothing for granted with such a creature. This enemy could be a tricky kill. It took some time for these fiends to regenerate, but it did not take them that long. Then I saw it.

It was happening quickly, already I saw his little finger moving, as if it was waiting to join the rest of the putrid flesh to come back to life. I had a theory about making sure that did not happen and I planned to put that theory to the test now. I knew I had to work fast. Quickly I got to work to make sure my enemy never regenerated again. There only seemed to be one way to make sure this did not happen. I did not relish it.

I sighed with disgust realizing the grim work that lay ahead. Work that must be done and that I must do myself here and now, right away. So I began the grim task. First I stripped Doom of his helmet and body armor and clothing. Then I got down to the grisly work at hand. I knew what I must do now as much as it repelled me to do it. I quickly lifted my sword speaking harshly to his corpse, "You can not regenerate if you are cut into different parts and they are kept separate and never united," I cried in rage and cursed him foully for what I must do now.

Then my sword fell down hard upon the body of my enemy, and I got down to the terrible work of dismembering the corpse of Lord Karlath Doom. Arms, legs, torso, head, were each quickly separated and kept apart. It was a strangely non-bloody event. It appeared Doom did not have blood as we know it to be—or very little of it. I wrapped up each piece of the corpse in Doom's own clothing making separate bundles.

Suddenly there was a loud noise at the end of the vast hallway that attracted my attention. Guards? Well if so, they were too late now, but I would fight them too if I had to!

I quickly looked up and saw the form of just one man entering the far end of the hallway. He was tall and bloody, holding a knife and a death ray weapon.

"Crooch?" I asked incredulously.

"Yes, it is I, Jon Kirk. Tob and Vakon are no more. They went down hard, but they went down and are now with their accursed ancestors," he stated as he walked over towards me. He was a bloody mess to see, as I am sure that I was also. He took in the scene at once, then nodded his approval.

"Lord Doom is dead." I told him simply.

"I see. B-but what have you done to his body, to the corpse?"

"I have taken him apart. To prevent him from regenerating. It was necessary. His body must be broken up and I will have the parts scattered to the four winds so they can never be united, and so they can never regenerate."

"How can you do that? We are not on a planet but in a warship in the void of outer space," Crooch replied, curious and showing some nervous stress. He looked at me fearfully when he realized the full measure of what I had just done to his master's body. He seemed almost as sacred of me at that moment, as he had been of Lord Doom. That was fine with me at that point.

"I will show you," I answered, wiping the blood from my face and hands and cleaning the blood from my sword upon Doom's own clothing. Then I picked up Doom's head, which I had taken outside of his helm, holding it up by his long hair. "Now, follow me to the bridge. I am taking this ship!"

Crooch looked at me nervously, then nodded and followed me to an elevator that took us to the upper level of the bridge of Lord Doom's Enemy Empire flagship. Once the elevator doors opened on the bridge we saw it was full of officers and specialists representing half a dozen races and worlds. They were all Enemy Empire crew. They looked aghast at the grisly trophy that they could plainly see that I carried in my hand, and all moved aside for me and out of my way. None gave me any challenge.

I calmly walked into the bridge holding up Lord Doom's severed head for all to see. "I am Jon Kirk, and Lord Doom is no more—and he is never coming back! I order you to surrender this ship and your fleet to the fleet of Admiral Quarto-Zar immediately! All opposition must stop now!"

Every face of every minion of Doom's crew on that bridge looked at me in absolute shock, and then they looked upon the severed head of Lord Doom that I held boldly in my hand, then they looked back at me with total fear and horror—but there were some others there I noticed who openly showed great relief at the sight of their dead master. So not all were loyal to the dead Sindalki lord. Good!

"Obey the Emperor's order now!" Crooch barked in angry command at the crew and they jumped to comply. All thoughts of resistance by them were gone now. "Do as Jon Kirk, Emperor of Worlds, orders you to do! Do it now!"

* * * *

Admiral Quarto-Zar had been fighting a brave holding action against the enemy fleet for hours with little hope of victory. He had been unable to stop or explode the black moon—in fact he had lost track of the moon in the fury of battle and it had escaped his vision, but he and his ships had never given up as they tried all they could to stop the enemy fleet. He had had some small success, his ships had done some damage to the enemy, hoping in vain that they had bought Ares some time, but they knew it had not been enough. Now he felt that the die was cast and that the fleet of Lord Doom was ready to administer the *coup de grace* and destroy all the ships remaining of his decimated fleet.

"Admiral, there is a comm coming over from the flagship of the Enemy Empire fleet," Commander Sala, communications officer advised his superior quickly.

Quarto-Zar folded his massive black wings back into the position of extreme sadness, anticipating news of the impending end of his fleet, or the image of a dead or dying Jon Kirk shown as prisoner upon the enemy flagship. "Put it through, commander."

There was some vision appearing, images on a screen from Lord Doom's ship, from the bridge apparently. Quarto-Zar looked closely and was rather surprised when he saw another Winged-man from Zar looking curiously at him. He knew this one, another Shorn such as he was, and most probably a *consignat* like himself as well, but one who was serving with the enemy. What did he want?

"Admiral Quarto-Zar, I am Kinto-Za, of the Zar nest hive Za, and foresworn Shorn believer. I offer you the surrender of the Enemy Empire fleet. Lord Doom is dead and the battle is over. We surrender to you, and all opposition by vessels under my command will cease immediately as ordered by Emperor Jon Kirk."

Quatro-Zar hardly knew what to say, so shocked was he by this sudden announcement. It was inconceivable! Amazing! Then he saw in the background of the enemy bridge a man standing tall and proud who looked very much like Jon Kirk, and he noticed in his emperor's hand that he appeared to be holding what looked to be a man's severed head. He recognized it as the head of the Sindalki traitor, Lord Karlath Doom!

Admiral Quarto nodded his massive head in a Shorn prayer. What he had prayed to come to pass, had somehow come to pass. He looked at the opposing admiral and allowed a grim smile of satisfaction.

"Yes, of course, Kinto-Za, my respects, and my officers will give you all the commands to have your vessels fall in line with our own. Prepare to accept our orders and coordinates."

"Yes, Admiral," was the reply from the Enemy Empire flagship, "we wait your orders and commands."

CHAPTER 20

Home and Back Again

"And that is how it happened," I told Sirah, along with Aron the Eldest, King Shamar, Zaor, Sahn-jor and all the other ministers, advisors, leaders and generals of my empire who had been gathered together to hear the results of the battle that had taken place far away by the black moon. "Lord Doom's body was cut apart so it can never be joined together again. I am sad to say that I saw to it personally, the pieces of his flesh were burned and then each one flung out into deep space in different directions. They shall travel millions of miles apart forever. They shall never unite. He is one creature that shall never be brought together again or regenerate. He is dead for sure now. Dead for all eternity."

There were many cheers of immense joy and great relief.

"But tell me, Lord Aron. Tell me what has happened here on Ares while I was gone. How were you and your people ever able to divert the black moon from colliding with Ares?" I asked astounded by the good news I had discovered when I saw that Ares was safe, and much relieved by it. For all of us in the fleet—even with our victory against Lord Doom—had lost contact with the black moon for we had been too late to overtake it, and assumed that it had already collided with Ares. We thought Ares was gone then, much as Earth and Sindalki were gone.

Lord Aron smiled warmly, "We found a way, Jon Kirk. There is always a way for victory. You above all have proved to us that fact is true."

"Where there is life, there is hope," I stated confidently.

"Where there is life, there is hope, Jon Kirk. You still live!"

"I still live!" I nodded at the compliment, then gave him a big smile, to let on to him that I understood the import of those words and that I was totally relieved that Ares was safe. My beloved Sirah, Alun my son, and all the people of Ares were alive and safe too now. I was overjoyed by the outcome of these events but this success could only make my thoughts turn to the sadness I still felt about the loss of the Earth. The death of my home world left an empty place of sadness that tugged at my heart and would forever be a source of pain and anger within me. It was a bitter realization.

"What is it that troubles you at such a joyous time as this, Jon Kirk?" Lord Kneth said to me, perhaps reading my inner feelings, as I am sure they must have mirrored his own.

With Lord Doom dead and gone, Lord Kneth was truly now the last of the Sindalki. He was the last of his noble race—as was I. It was a most sobering thought. I knew why he had asked me the question, for I knew that he felt my inner pain and the loss I felt at the destruction of the Earth. It was my silent inner loss that I held tightly within my tortured heart, but he wanted me to say it verbally, to get it out in the open.

"You know." I stated in a low tone, trying to hide my sadness. I spoke in a soft whisper, "You above all know, Lord Kneth."

"Yes, indeed I do, and I shall carry the death of the Sindalki with me for the rest of my life," he said expressing great sadness and guilt. Then he looked at me closely and said with a sharp look in his eyes, "but you need not carry the death of Earth forever, Jon Kirk. Earth is not Sindalki. While I would no longer have what was done to Sindalki prevented—for it is better for all what has been done remain done—it is not the same case with the Earth. Earth need not remain destroyed."

I looked at Lord Kneth with evident surprise, then utter astonishment. What was he implying? I looked to Aron the Eldest and he just nodded at me with a slim smile that seemed to verify Kneth's words. I hardly knew what to say.

"It is a new universe now, a better one, thanks to you, Jon Kirk," Lord Kneth continued.

I nodded, I thanked him, but I did not know exactly what he was trying to get at.

"But I must ask you now a very serious question. Do you want to reverse the process that led to the destruction of your Earth?"

I looked hard at the Sindalki lord. Had I heard him correctly? It seemed incomprehensible. I looked at him in shock. "What do you mean?"

"What I mean is this. There is a way that the evil that has been done, may be undone. Earth is destroyed, but it need not *remain* destroyed. There is a way that the planet's destruction can be prevented—like it never happened."

"Truly? How can that be done?" I asked astonished by his words and the promise and hope that they held for me.

Aron the Eldest spoke up now, "Jon Kirk, with Lord Kneth's help, we have been able to master some of the aspects of the kingdom of time. We are now able to go back into the past, by harnessing the power and knowledge of time and space. It is possible for us to send an individual back into the past to the moment before Lord Doom destroyed the Earth—so that he might be able to prevent Doom's destruction of the Earth from ever happening in the first place. It can be done."

I looked at Lord Aron and Lord Kneth in disbelief but with growing hope in my heart. "Is such a thing truly possible?"

"Yes, it is, however it is not an easy procedure, and it has serious dangers, possible conflicting consequences, but it is certainly possible," Lord Aron stated confidently.

"Then let us do it! Let us do it as soon as it can be done!" I stated with eager determination. "I want to save the Earth if it can be done. I want to prevent it from being destroyed if possible. I want to save those people. What do I have to do?"

Lord Aron slowly explained. "Now, with Lord Doom's total and true death—a death he shall never awaken from—it is a far simpler matter for us to send someone back into the past to confront him—his previous past self—and then stop him in his destruction of the Earth. It is possible now. All we need is a man to send back to stop Lord Doom. You are that man. Are you interested, Jon Kirk?"

"You know that I am!" I stated sharply, impatiently.

"Then know this," Lord Kneth explained to me in a stern voice, "we will send you back to Lord Doom's ship exactly where and when it was in orbit around the Earth—and there you must kill him before he gives the order to the crew of his ship to destroy the planet. Killing Doom's earlier self will be difficult, but a far simpler matter than if he still lived in our time and still possessed all of his many dark powers. However, while you will be fighting with a past shade of his former self, he will still be powerful even though he has succumbed to a true and eternal death here in our present time. This past Lord Doom will now be substantially less powerful than the two previous versions you have fought, defeated, and already killed. Since he is already dead in the future—which is our present—there can be no time complications by his death now here in the past. There is no way he can prevent you from acting against him—or no way for him go back in time to undo what you will go into the past to undo. But be forewarned, he is still a deadly dangerous adversary. Extremely treacherous."

"I know that," I answered my mind bursting with growing excitement to get into action again now and to stop Lord Doom.

"Then are you ready, Jon Kirk?" Lord Aron asked me in a more sharp but ominous tone. For I knew this was a deadly gamble—but a gamble I was ready and willing to take.

"Am I ever! Yes, of course I am ready!" I stated boldly anxious, eager to take on this most important mission. I kissed my beloved Sirah, goodbye, telling her, "I shall see you again soon, my love."

"Come home to me after you save your Earth, my love," she whispered softly.

Then I was lead away by Ras-noor, Aron and Lord Kneth and placed into Tar-gool's ancient transfer machine as his technicians prepared me to go on my next most dangerous mission—*to travel back in time to save the Earth from eternal Doom!*

ABOUT THE AUTHOR

GARY LOVISI is a Brooklyn-based author and science fiction fan who was inspired early in life by the John Carter of Mars books—and all the great works of Edgar Rice Burroughs—which he first read as a teenager in the 1960s. In his Jon Kirk of Ares Chronicles, he seeks to capture the sense of wonder, rousing pulse-pounding action, and strange adventures on alien worlds, that made Burroughs' classic books so much fun to read. Lovisi has written in all genres of fiction, from short stories to novels; and non-fiction about authors, artists, and book collecting. He edits *Paperback Parade* magazine and founded Gryphon Books. He was short-listed for a Mystery Writers of America Edgar Award for the Best Short Story of the Year, and received a Spur Award from the Western Writers of America. Lovisi's first Jon Kirk of Ares novel, *The Winged-Men* was published by Wildside Press in 2014. His next two original novels in the series came out in 2015 from Wildside Press: *The Invisible Men* (#2) and *The Space Men* (#3). The Jon Kirk of Ares Chronicles is off and running, with books #4 and #5 out now, more original novels planned. To find out more about Lovisi, his writing, other books, or Jon Kirk of Ares Chronicles news, check his Facebook page or his website: www.gryphonbooks.com.

ABOUT THE COVER ARTIST

MARCUS BOAS is a New York City illustrator, and a master of vivid fantasy and science fiction art. His use of striking colors and heroic images in his art dazzles all who view it. His stunning work has been a mainstay used on the covers of many books and magazines in the fantasy field over his decades long art career. A big fan of Edgar Rice Burroughs, and especially the John Carter of Mars series, Marcus is a natural to do the covers for the Jon Kirk of Ares Chronicles.

He has created wonderful cover art for the first three books in the Jon Kirk of Ares series and now created original cover art especially for this new edition. You can see some of his outstanding work collected in such books as *Heroic Fantasy*, *Jungle*, and others published by Kaso Comics at www.kasocomics.com. Wonderful prints are available for some of his beautiful work.

ABOUT THE MAPMAKER

LUCILLE CALI is a Brooklyn, New York free-lance artist whose map of Ares is based upon the original map first drawn by the author in 1971, when he wrote the first book in the Jon Kirk of Ares Chronicles. Her latest star map takes in all the vast area and worlds of the Known Universe that take place in the Jon Kirk of Ares Chronicles. Cali has done numerous covers for various Gryphon Books, as well as issues of *Hardboiled* magazine and is a very talented and versatile artist.

www.ingramcontent.com/pod-product-compliance
Lightning Source LLC
Chambersburg PA
CBHW020650180626
46816CB00003B/1210